Lily B.
on the
Brink of
Cool

ELIZABETH CODY KIMMEL

Lily B.
on the
Brink of
Cool

SCHOLASTIC INC.
New York Toronto London Auckland Sydney
Mexico City New Delhi Hong Kong Buenos Aires

ISBN 0-439-68356-4

12 11 10 9 8 7 6 5 4 3 2 1   6 7 8 9/0

Printed in the U.S.A.   40

First Scholastic printing, September 2004

Typography by Amy Ryan

Lily B.
on the
Brink of
Cool

Wednesday, June 19
My room.

NOTE TO FUTURE BIOGRAPHERS: Welcome to the notebook of the soon-to-be internationally recognized writer Lily Blennerhassett (that's me—nom de plume pending). I am recording my life for the benefit of future scholars devoting their professional lives to my Collected Works and for the benefit of readers, writers, and all who Seek the Truth.

And also because this counts as a summer project for Advanced English.

Thursday, June 20
Kitchen Table. With Nutter Butter.

My life lacks excitement. It's worse than that, actually. My life lacks action. Conflict. Drama. My life lacks anything of substance, unless you count three green and two yellow vegetable portions on that nutritional food pyramid. The rich and varied scope of human experience has passed me by. I am an uninteresting person. I lack the raw materials necessary to produce a great novel.

I blame my parents. They are simple, plain, by-the-book people. They do not take risks. They do not pick up hitchhikers. They do not sample mushrooms that grow in the wild. They are so mainstream, they make The First Lady look radical.

Take driving with my father, for example. I may be only thirteen, and totally lacking in driver's education, but even I know that on the highway the left lane is supposed to be the fast lane. But my father disregards this Accepted Fact of Life on a daily basis. He'll maneuver the Honda into the left lane, then cruise along at 55, the posted speed limit in most of New York State. Not 54. Never 56. And when regular people, nice average Joes, come up behind him wanting to pass, he refuses to move over to the right lane. And okay, some of these people might get a little irritated. And maybe they flash their

2

lights, or honk, or do a little innocent tailgating. Can you blame them? And what does my father do? Nothing at all. Just chugs along at 55 with this quiet It's a Beautiful Day in the Neighborhood expression on his face. And if you make the mistake of pointing out that someone is trying to pass, he'll just shake his head and smile. He'll point to the speedometer. He'll say, "I'm doing the legal speed limit. Nobody has any right to complain. This is the speed we're supposed to be going."

I think I've made my point.

But let's not forget my mother. Somebody ought to apply for a grant to seriously study her. When my mother stays in a hotel, she *makes the beds* in the morning. I am not inventing this. Whether it's the ritziest place in the state or the Super 8 just off the freeway exit ramp, she always makes the beds and folds the used towels neatly on the rack. She claims she "can't think clearly with the beds unmade." I may only have gotten a B in bio, but I do know there is no connection between brain activity and bed sheets. I don't need therapy to know the real issue is how our family appears to other people. Unmade beds are untidy, and the last thing Mom wants is for word to get out to the Super 8 housekeeping staff that the Blennerhassetts from Room 118 are Untidy People.

Given the opportunity, I feel sure William Shakespeare would have driven faster than the speed limit. And I feel very safe in saying that Jane Austen would not, in comparable circumstances, have straightened up her room at the Super 8.

Life in the fast lane has NEVER been worse.

Friday, June 21
Raining. Upstairs. Window seat.

I am waiting for Charlotte. It will be difficult saying a serious good-bye to someone who is attending Young Executive Camp for part of the summer. If it had been anyone else, I would have written a sarcastic short story about it and submitted it to *The New Yorker*. But it is more complicated than that.

Charlotte and I have spent every summer together since we were in kindergarten and became best friends. First it was Fairy Day Camp, then it was Sports Center Intensive Swim Program. Somewhere around the third or fourth grade we did the Brownie/Girl Scout thing. And for the last several years Camp Migawam. We slept in a cabin together, canoed together, swam together, launched butter pats at the ceiling in the dining room. Together.

I realize it isn't Charlotte's fault, necessarily, that Camp Migawam went out of business after Charlotte called the newspaper regarding the offering of bribes by camp administrators to the state health and safety inspector. I don't blame her for that. But when it came time for us to pick a new way to spend the summer, Charlotte got all flipped out about this new alternative camp she'd found out about on the web, where Chief Executive Officers and Business Tycoons of tomorrow come together for the purposes of "educational enrichment." I looked at the brochure, just to see. It was appalling! No canoes. No cabins. No swimming, no sailing, no archery, not even any nature walks. Instead, the brochure talked about seminars, interactive workshops, and lectures by visiting corporate leaders. In short, it was a nightmare.

I kept thinking she'd come to her senses. I kept thinking we'd find some nice tennis camp, or a riding program, or a hiking trip for girls. But Charlotte wouldn't budge. She was determined to enroll in Young Executive Camp. Spending a large part of the summer without Charlotte would be a disaster. But let's face it—me at Young Executive Camp would be a *catastrophe*.

My future plans do not include working in an office. They do not include panty hose and unscuffed shoes. They do not include briefcases or cell phones. They do not include carefully folded newspapers and takeout coffee or the commuter train.

I am going to be a writer. And if circumstances become difficult, and my genius is not immediately recognized, and it becomes unpleasantly necessary for me to take on some additional work, there are several jobs I feel qualified for and interested in (in which I feel interested and for which I feel qualified?) (for and in which I feel qualified and interested? Future Biographers: You decide).

JOBS I WOULD TAKE:

1) Shower Taker. Duties include testing variety of plumbing hardware by taking long, hot showers, evaluating water pressure, durability, and ease of use.

2) TV Blurb Writer. Duties include viewing television shows and writing brief (under five words) synopsis of plot to appear in the local television listings section of newspapers.

3) Award Ceremony Seat Filler. Duties include occupying the seats of celebrities at award shows while they are accepting awards or visiting the facilities. Check your sources—this is a real job! Clothes to be provided by network.

So you understand, Future Biographers, why I cannot go to camp with Charlotte, despite of the fact that we are breaking a lifelong tradition, despite the fact that I will be left alone with my sadly unexciting parents, and despite the fact that my parents have found no suitable alternative to Camp Migawam at this late date and have only very grudgingly allowed me to stay home because of my persuasive and persistent argument that this notebook, my Advanced English summer project, will require all my free time and, once completed, will virtually guarantee my place on the Honor Roll. And I only agreed to write down these *highly* confidential things because I simply have to show my English teacher that I have kept this notebook, and am not required to allow anyone to actually read it. That's a privilege I'm saving for you, Future Biographers.

(Note to self: possible title for first novel—*Charlotte's Story: Of Finks and Friends*.)

Postlude:

Well. Charlotte and I had our traditional taco and root beer dinner. Her parents picked her up a half hour early (unfair!) because she has to leave so early in the morning. There wasn't even time to throw a few darts at the Britney Spears poster on the back of my door. It was all over so fast. Charlotte was here, and now she's gone. I'm alone now, except for you Future Biographers. Do you guys like tacos?

I'm in a bad mood.

Saturday, June 22
The Honda.

I am in the backseat of the car enduring today's Family Outing (hereafter F.O.). It will be important for you to note that F.O.s are a significant part of my upbringing. My prediction is that it will take years of therapy to undo the psychological damage I've suffered during these excursions. My mother is the Evil Architect of these outings, but my father bears equal blame for his enthusiastic support of them. F.O.s, by maternal law, are required to 1) be educational; 2) force the attendee to speak in hushed tones and wear sensible clothes; 3) attract primarily pale, underweight people wearing socks under their sandals; 4) dim the already bleak social prospects of all attendees under the age of 16. Possibly 40.

For your files, let me consult the F.O. Hall of Fame roster. There was the yarn-making seminar with picnic lunch last fall. Two years ago we attended the History of Tea festival. I have toured the facilities of the state's only accordion manufacturer. I have assembled my own cornhusk doll while listening to a musical documentation of the history of American folk fiddle tunes. Please, don't make me continue.

Today's F.O. is to the grand opening of Maple Village, one of those reconstructed colonial villages where college students with asymmetrical haircuts and glow-in-the-dark Swatches wear polyester imitations of 18th century clothing, and stand around making candles and soap. My only consolation is that I will not be humiliated like these students, who are forced to act out embarrassing colonial domestic duties while others watch.

10:57 a.m. My mother MADE ME CHURN BUTTER!

12:10 p.m. If you're going to go to all the trouble of making a "three-dimensional acre of living history accurate down to the smallest detail," as it says right here in the Maple Village brochure, then explain to me how it follows that there is a cappuccino bar by the picnic area.

3:47 p.m. I am tired, humiliated, and completely fed up with 18th-century kitchen utensils. The backseat of the Honda has never felt so good.

9:45 p.m. I am really, really mad at Charlotte McGrath.

Sunday, June 23
Bedroom. Eavesdropping on parents downstairs through heating vent.

8:29 a.m. Years of mornings monitoring conversations through the vent may finally be paying off. Something is up, Future Biographers!

8:30 a.m. I'm hearing the name Delia. (The heating vent gives me only a 50% accurate version of conversations).

8:32 a.m. There it is again, The Delia Drop. I'm sure the Blennerhassett Institute (when it is founded) will have all this family information, Future Biographers (may I call you F.B.s? It's easier to write). But for your ease and research convenience, I'll divulge Delia's identity. She's my mother's brother's daughter (read: NOT A BLENNERHASSETT). I see her on holidays, mostly. She gives age-inappropriate gifts (last Christmas she gave me a set of Little Mermaid paints). She arrives late and leaves early to go back to work (she's a lawyer). She makes and receives numerous calls to and from clients on her cell phone, even at the dinner table (she's a workaholic). And from what I can tell, a large portion of her life is about food. Avoiding it, getting fat-free versions of it, running to the gym to work it off. It's insane. The woman is a size 2. I've seen bigger hips on PEZ dispensers.

8:35 a.m. Delia is apparently buying some webbing. Maybe she's going to start a side business making dog leashes? Or harnesses? What else can you do with webbing? Fishing nets?

8:37 a.m. The webbing is apparently causing quite a bit of excitement. My mother is talking so fast, I can hardly make out what she's saying.

8:39 a.m. Apparently this is very expensive webbing. How many feet of webbing is she buying? How many leashes can one very skinny girl make?

8:41 a.m. My mother and father seem to be agreeing that Delia is getting harried. The webbing project must be overwhelming her.

8:42 a.m. Oh.

8:43 a.m. *Oh.*

8:44 a.m. OH.

8:45 a.m. I had thought now that Charlotte's gone, I'd hit rock bottom immediately and stay there. But apparently I'm going to plunge even lower. Delia is getting *married*, and it sounds like the Blennerhassetts will be attending the *wedding*. Forget everything you've read, because unless maybe it's your own, a wedding is the most boring thing in the universe. I know. I went to one two years ago—my mother's hairdresser married a shampoo and conditioner sales rep—and I still get flashbacks when I walk past a salon. They served ravioli over rice. The bridesmaids wore pastel taffeta. The band played "If You're Happy and You Know It, Clap Your Hands." We were forced to participate in a conga line! Is it possible for me to develop strep throat simply by wanting it very very badly?

Monday, June 24
The Dress Barn. Young Miss section. Changing room.

The horrors of clothes shopping. Where does my mother find these things? She whisks into the dressing room and hands me items triumphantly, like she's Donatella Versace previewing her new line. The only thing is, the outfits she's bringing in for me to try on look like they were made for one of those American Girl dolls. Ruffly stuff. High collars. Puffed sleeves. Like I'm getting ready for a *Masterpiece Theatre* audition. Who wants to walk around looking like they were sucked into some giant, girl-eating doily?

1:15 p.m. I won't try that on.

1:16 p.m. SHE CAN'T MAKE ME TRY THAT ON.

1:20 p.m. My self-esteem has never been lower. I can hardly bring myself to write about it. It was . . . shiny. Green. Lace collar, poofed-out skirt. An ABOMINATION. A lampshade with sleeves. The only way to get her to take it away was to try it on. I made sure to slouch and hunch over so that it wouldn't fit right. After all, my mother is a reasonable person. Clearly she could see that with me inside it, the dress was . . . awful. Tonight I'll call Charlotte, and we'll laugh about it. It *is* kind of funny. Some poor soul actually designed that dress, and maybe even took it home to show their mom. Charlotte will bust a gut laughing. No one appreciates a fashion disaster quite like Charlotte.

1:30 p.m. My mother BOUGHT the dress. She said it will be perfect for the wedding. She said I will look "darling."

Charlotte must never, *never* know about this.

Tuesday, June 25
The dinner table. Stony silence.

6:15 p.m. All I did, and I think F.B.s will agree it was a reasonable inquiry, was to ask why we didn't know about this wedding sooner? I'm no expert, but aren't you generally given more than two days to get outfitted, buy a present, reserve your hotel room, and get driving directions from Triple A? It just seems strange, that's all, that we didn't receive the invitation sooner. Say, in March.

6:20 p.m. My mother says Delia is very busy and it is inappropriate to ask these questions and they are certainly not in the spirit of the occasion and we're delighted to be asked and why quibble over timing and what difference does it make, for heaven's sake, since we would have said yes anyway and let's all just stop talking about it and would anyone like some more asparagus.

6:25 p.m. My father says, very quietly, that we are "B list."

6:26 p.m. Unable to contain myself, I ask for an explanation.

6:27 p.m. My father says that after all the "A list" people have been invited, if some of them say they can't attend, the "B list" people then get invitations.

6:28 p.m. I suggest, given the very late date, that perhaps we are the "F List."

6:29 p.m. I'm going to experiment with remaining silent for a while.

Wednesday, June 26

First-floor coat closet. Phone cord under door.
Bad smell from someone's rain boots.

CHARLOTTE: Charlotte McGrath's line.

ME: Finally! I've been trying for two days and nobody answers—don't they give you receptionists at Young Executive Camp? Voice mail?

CHARLOTTE *(becoming nasal and officelike)*: To whom am I speaking?

ME *(putting on German accent)*: Zis is Herr Klimt from ze department of cleanliness. Ve heff received complaints about a bad smell comink from your room, Fräulein.

(Long pause. Charlotte giggles.)

ME AND CHARLOTTE: Hello?

(Long, pant-wetting laughter)

ME: Seriously, where have you been? I've been trying to get you forever.

CHARLOTTE: We went on an orientation trip to learn how to communicate with and trust one another.

ME: Let me guess—you had to stand on a platform with your eyes closed and fall backward so the others could catch you.

(Pause.)

CHARLOTTE: You make it sound less exciting than it actually was.

ME: What's next? Bungee jumping for risk-management skills?

CHARLOTTE: What a great idea! I'm going to recommend it to my team leader. A new camper came this morning, Lil. I'll bet it's not too late for you to enroll.

ME: Believe me, it's too late, Char. Delia's getting married and I'm going to her wedding in an awful green dress. Are there any prelaw campers there? I thought maybe there might be some legal precedent allowing me to refuse to wear the dress, you know. Some sort of Fashion Sanctuary Law, or something.

CHARLOTTE: I'll ask around. My team leader says weddings bring some of the most widespread networking opportunities available.

ME: I don't want to network, Char. I don't want to work, period. I want to go canoeing and sit around the campfire making s'mores and singing the old songs. I want to tell the story about the escaped madman with the hook for a right hand who stalks couples on Lovers' Lane. I want to call Kool-Aid bug juice.

CHARLOTTE: How's the summer project for English class coming?

ME: I'm writing down every word we say as we say it.

CHARLOTTE: Spleen. Toe jam. Calamari.

ME: Writing 'em down.

CHARLOTTE: Ectoplasm. Worm boy.

ME: Writing. Got it. How's your bunkhouse?

CHARLOTTE: It's a dormitory, Lily.

ME: We've got to get you out of there.

CHARLOTTE: I don't want to get out of here, Lily. Why don't you come? It's going to be so great! I have four seminars to choose from every day. I receive a complimentary *Wall Street Journal* each morning at breakfast. I'm making important contacts with other young executives that will one day be incredibly valuable to me. Not to mention how impressive this will look on my college applications.

ME: You're thirteen, Char. College is something like ten years away.

CHARLOTTE: Five. Four if I graduate early. Not much time in a supercompetitive world. Everyone's going after the same spots, and let me tell you, there are some pretty smart kids around. My roommate, for example. She speaks three languages, has perfect pitch, composes original works for the cello, and turned down a summer scholarship to the American Ballet Theatre School to be here.

ME: Well. You know. If you're impressed by that sort of thing. It's not like she's written a book or something.

CHARLOTTE: Actually—

ME: I DON'T WANT TO KNOW!

(Brief silence.)

CHARLOTTE: I was just going to say she'd like to do that

someday. But I'm sure she won't. I mean, not just any-body can pick up a pen and write. You have to be special. You have to be gifted. You have to be born to it.

ME *(happily—Charlotte sure knows how to casually sling the praise-by-proxy)*: I wish you'd come home, Char. This summer is going to suck!

CHARLOTTE : You could give Y.E.C. a chance, couldn't you?

ME: YEC to you, YUK to me. Be honest, Char. If you were the one at home, and I was away at Junior Prose-and-Poetry-Writing Camp, would you sign up even though you hate creative writing just because I was there?

CHARLOTTE *(sighing)*: No. Anyway, it isn't for the whole summer. I'll be back in three weeks.

ME: Three weeks is forever. You have to swear to come over the second you get back.

CHARLOTTE : Tacos and root beer?

ME: Tacos and root beer.

CHARLOTTE : I promise, Lil. Listen, I have to go meet my Web Possibilities Think Tank partner.

ME: Okay, then. Give her my best. Have lots of fun, ha ha.

CHARLOTTE : Him. I will.

(Very long silence.)

ME: Boys?

CHARLOTTE : What?

ME: Boys. Boys? Camper boys? You're meeting boys?

CHARLOTTE : It's coed, yeah.

ME *(slapping my hand to my forehead in despair)*: Are you going to get a boyfriend, Charlotte? We swore we'd find boyfriends together!!

CHARLOTTE : I don't think I'm going to get a boyfriend, Lil, really.

ME *(practically wailing)*: But you might! You could! I'll never catch up with you!

CHARLOTTE : The guys are mostly pinheads, Lily. Slide rules and thick glasses.

ME *(with self-pitying sigh)*: Life is finally going to leave me in the dust this summer.

CHARLOTTE : I really, really have to go, Lily. Don't worry, okay? I promise to have as little fun as possible.

ME *(sniffing)*: Really?

CHARLOTTE : Really.

ME: Well, okay then.

Thursday, June 27
Sanctuary. (My room.)

MEMO

To: The Department of Blossoming Author Protective
  Services

From: Lily Blennerhassett

Dear Sir or Madam:

I am writing to alert you to a serious violation of
B.A.P.S. protocol currently in process in the
Blennerhassett home. As your files will indicate, current
blossoming author and future world-renowned writer
Lily Blennerhassett has resided at this address for
approximately ten of her thirteen years. Said blossoming
author is being Significantly Hampered and forced to
remain an Uninteresting Person by a stifling and
uncreative home life.

CURRENT VIOLATIONS INCLUDE:
1) Dangerous levels of exposure to the History
Channel and Animal Planet television stations.
2) Inappropriately dull meals with overemphasis on
nutritional content and savagely boring dining
conversation.

3) Hazardously damaging fashion environment including frequent appearances of wide-wale corduroys and shirts with ruffly collars.

4) Required presence at impending wedding of unattractively slender relative.

It is the opinion of this informant that the continuation of these violations will result in a significant level of creative erosion in said blossoming author, which may well hamper her efforts to produce a first novel worthy of the National Book Award. This informant urges B.A.P.S. to immediately take all appropriate action to correct the violations occurring in the Blennerhassett home, if not for the sake of humanity, then for the future of the American Literary Institution.

Friday, June 28

Hour of departure for wedding approaches.

11:32 a.m. The Lampshade with Sleeves has been secured in garment bag and placed in Honda. Sadly, the chances of this dress being lost, damaged, or mutilated before the wedding are growing even slimmer than Delia.

11:50 a.m. Keys to the Honda missing.

11:59 a.m. Lunch being served—fat-free turkey on whole-grain bread, apple slices, vegetable juice.

12:31 p.m. Frequent commands for all Blennerhassetts to visit the bathroom before departure continue to be issued.

12:40 p.m. Keys to Honda still missing.

12:48 p.m. Last bag placed in trunk. Road-map collection placed in glove compartment. Lunch dishes cleared away, scoured, and sterilized. Table and kitchen surfaces rubbed violently with antibacterial cleanser.

12:50 p.m. Keys to Honda still missing.

12:55 p.m. Final house check occurring—lights out, coffee machine unplugged, windows locked, shades down, all faucets and water-bearing devices firmly in the off position, beds made neatly (so that any thieves breaking and entering during our absence will not think the Blennerhassetts are Untidy People).

12:59 p.m. Keys to the Honda located in my bathroom behind the soap dish. Discussion ensues as to how they got there. No explanation is forthcoming. I suggest the whole episode be filed under L, for Life's Little Mysteries, right next to the Loch Ness Monster.

Backseat of Honda.

2:30 p.m. Note to self—when legally adult (18? 21?), vow never again to tolerate the playing of Broadway's greatest hits on any car trip.

3:10 p.m. Wrong exit taken from freeway. Parents exhibiting signs of nervous agitation and veiled hostility.

3:26 p.m. Back on freeway.

3:37 p.m. Correct exit spotted, but accidentally passed.

3:45 p.m. Back on freeway.

3:50 p.m. Exit relocated and taken. Hotel in sight.

5:55 p.m. Well, it's a fancy place anyway. Two-bedroom suite means two enormous beds for Mom to make tomorrow morning. Plush carpet. Coffeemaker in the bathroom. Attractive mahogany wardrobe that opens to reveal wide-screen television set. No time to ponder the origins of the rehearsal dinner, as we are expected at Olivieri's Trattoria down the street for said ritual in thirty-five minutes. From what I can pick up, I understand it's a traditional, night-before-the-wedding dinner where all the relatives show up, possibly to make sure the whole gang can get through three hours in one another's company without resorting to verbal or physical abuse.

The unimportant relatives' table; Olivieri's Trattoria, rehearsal dinner.

6:37 p.m.

AUNT TIFFY: And is this Lily? Can I believe my eyes?
(I look around helplessly, hoping another Lily is standing behind me and clothed in something better than the mock turtleneck and striped skirt I am unhappily wearing.)

AUNT TIFFY: Let me look at you! Don't you look darling!
(This cannot be said for Aunt Tiffy, who resembles a marshmallow sporting an inexpensive wig.)

ME *(mumbling)*: Thank you.

AUNT TIFFY: Stand up. Let me get a really good look at you.
(I am speechless, paralyzed with horror.)

MOM: Lily? Did you hear your Aunt Tiffy? Stand up, honey.
(I am still speechless, rising to feet on numb legs.)

AUNT TIFFY: Oh! For goodness' sake, the girl has grown two inches since Thanksgiving. And what a darling figure! Ted, come look at our Lily!

ME *(plummeting back into sitting position before Uncle Ted appears)*: Ack.

AUNT TIFFY: What did you say, dear?

MOM: Speak up, Lily. *(To the waiter)* Are there any whole-grain rolls?

AUNT TIFFY: Now where has Ted gone off to? Oh, but there's Chipper. Chipper! Chipper! Come over here and look at our Lily. She's turned into a real little lady.

(Possible tactics: 1) fake seizure 2) fake stomach virus 3) fake headache 4) reveal true feelings about Aunt Tiffy to Aunt Tiffy.)

6:50 p.m. Saved! Saved by the arrival of the first course! Mom and Aunt Tiffy have been distracted by nutritional concerns and are attempting to summon the chef to find out if the vegetable terrine can be removed, reassembled into its original vegetable form, and steamed.

6:52 p.m. Oh, F.B.s, it is even worse than I thought. A blizzard of bad dresses and clip-on ties. An accordion player is following people around, playing something that sounds like an optimistic Eastern European funeral march. Aunt Tiffy has abandoned her vegetable terrine in an attempt to find more relatives to assist in humiliating me.

SOME NOTABLE STATISTICS:

Average age of wedding guests: 50.

Average dress size: 16.

Average occupation: Men—public relations consultant. Women—*Ladies' Home Journal* subscriber.

Average condition of hair: Men—limp comb-over.

Women—ten inches over top of head.

Most commonly used adjective: Men—"terrific."
Women—"darling."

Most commonly asked question: Men—"How are
you liking school?" Women—"How are you liking
school?"

HELP ME!!!!!

7:00 p.m. Main course. Meat lumps that have died
trying to fight their way out of the gravy.

A ripple has gone through the room. F.B.s, hark! A
ripple! An Event in Progress! I am craning my neck to see
what is happening. No, I can't see. I'm standing. Aunt
Tiffy is pointing at me and calling Uncle Ted and
Chipper, who's fled to the men's room. But . . .

Oh, I see. Some people have mistakenly come in for
dinner. That caused the ripple. I guess no one told them
the restaurant was closed for a private party. They obviously don't belong at THIS wedding. They look way too
cool. They're all GORGEOUS! Looks like a mom, dad,
and daughter. Tan, and slim, and tall. Run! Run for your
lives, Cool People!

7:03 p.m. This is very strange. The Cool People are sitting down at an empty table. Have they lost their senses?
Don't they realize they could be CONTAMINATED by

the lethal levels of middle-American-averageness flooding the room?

7:05 p.m. They don't even look real. They're way too perfect for that. The woman is wearing this amazing dress that's like a tie-dyed tank-top shirt stretched into a dress. And she's got those blunt bangs and long straight hair—let me tell you, she looks like she just tumbled out of *Vogue*. And the man is buff and really handsome—he's wearing black on black. You know, black tie, black shirt, black suit. Now there is your sophisticated but understated look for the new age. There's a guy who commands RESPECT.

And the girl. I don't even know what to say. I'm struck dumb by my own inadequacy in comparison (though considering the parents I have to work with, we can all agree I never had a PRAYER). She has waist-length black hair (waist length! Imagine!). She's got perfect posture, and flawless makeup, and I'll bet all the champagne from my future National Book Award dinner that's a Donna Karan dress she's wearing. This girl makes the entire world look frumpy! Do people like this actually exist? Or did they just wander off a movie set?

My parents are speaking in hushed tones. I hate it when they speak in hushed tones. They are so obvious about it. Like they are rehearsing a play, and a director said, "Put your heads together and speak in hushed tones." I mean, when has anyone ever been interested in what they're saying ANYWAY?

Urgggh, I can't make out a word they are saying. I must resort to extreme measures.

A Little Dialogue:

ME: Aunt Tiffy?

AUNT TIFFY: Yes, dear?

ME: Who are those people who just came in?

AUNT TIFFY *(becoming very interested in straightening her lace collar)*: Hmmm?

ME: That family that just came in—over there. Who are they?

AUNT TIFFY: I didn't notice, sweetheart.

ME: But look. They're right there.

AUNT TIFFY: I think you had better speak to your mother about that.

(Speak to my mother? Does Aunt Tiffy think I am using code for "Tell me about how babies are made, please"?)

The Cool People have managed to obtain three salads, instead of the vegetable gloop and the defeated meat morsels. The waiter looks so relieved to see interesting and hip-looking people, I think he might actually sit down and join them.

Uncle Ted has reappeared at the table long enough to

whisk away his glass to the bar. Chipper never did return from the men's room. And Aunt Tiffy appears to have lapsed into some sort of functioning coma. WILL NO ONE TELL ME WHO THESE PEOPLE ARE?

Some Additional Dialogue:

ME: Mom?
　(*No response.*)
ME: Mom?
　(*No response.*)
ME: MOOOM! DAD!!
　(*Parents both look at me as if I have spontaneously
　grown a third eye.*)
DAD: Did you say something, honey?
ME: I was just wondering who those people are. The ones who just came in. Over there.
　(*Parents look at each other, not in the direction I am
　pointing.*)
ME: See? Them. The beautiful people. You can't miss them. Do you know who they are?
　(*Parents continue looking at each other. I find this
　deeply irritating.*)
ME: Fine. I guess I'll have to go over and ask them.
DAD: No, no, you stay right here. They're . . . distant relations.

ME *(faint and thoroughly stunned with disbelief)*: Relations? As in relatives? I share DNA with those people?

MOM: Distant, Lily. Cousins of cousins, I think it is.

ME: Well, family is family, right? They shouldn't be sitting all by themselves. I'm going to ask them to join us.

DAD *(grabbing my sleeve)*: No, no, you're not.

MOM : Sit down please, Lily.

ME: What? Why? What are you talking about?

(Parents resume looking at each other.)

ME *(employing a verbal strategy I know my parents can't stand)*: HELLOOOOOOOO!

MOM : We're enjoying some nice family time, that's all.

ME *(employing another expression I know they hate)*: Come again?

DAD: It really isn't appropriate to tangle with the seating arrangements. Delia put a great deal of thought into them, I'm sure.

ME: Are you avoiding those people?

MOM : We aren't avoiding anyone.

DAD: But we'd just rather not talk to them.

ME *(almost beside myself with the thrill of this unexpected Skeleton in the Closet)*: Why? Who are they? What happened? When? What went on?

(My mother presses her lips together to indicate that the subject is permanently closed.)

That was the highlight of the evening, F.B.s. And I never even found out their names. The rest of the dinner was death by boredom, with brief comic interludes. The fire alarm went off. Pandemonium followed. Rumor has it Uncle Ted filled his glass once too often, got a little confused, and pulled the fire alarm thinking it was the lever for a hidden panel that would open to reveal a secret room in the back of the restaurant.

The important thing to note is that in all the rushing and hubbub, the Cool People disappeared, and my parents have continued to change the subject every time I ask about them.

I WILL PERSEVERE! I WILL FIND THE COOL PEOPLE AND ROUT OUT THE TRUTH! I WILL NOT REST UNTIL I DO!

Maybe first I will rest a little. Good night.

Saturday, June 29

Hotel room. Prebreakfast activity.

8:27 a.m. My mother is making the beds.

8:40 a.m. My mother is wiping down the damp surfaces in the bathroom.

9:00 a.m. My mother is refolding the towels, and then she says we can go downstairs and have breakfast.

10:02 a.m. I have put on the green dress and resemble radioactive sofa cover.

10:49 a.m. Off to the church to hear wedding bells, etc., etc., etc.

11:14 a.m. I am sitting with the Cool People. The girl is wearing a turquoise beaded halter-top dress—I think Gwyneth Paltrow wore one like that to the Oscars. I was looking at them when they came into the church, and they sat right next to me! My mother looked horrified, but the organist started playing and it was too late for her to say anything.

11:16 a.m. I am writing very small so they cannot read what I am writing.

11:18 a.m. I AM SITTING WITH THE COOL PEOPLE!!

11:19 a.m. Am I being uncool by writing right now?

11:20 a.m. Apparently the organist only has a learner's permit to play. Many odd notes being struck.

11:22 a.m. Delia the bride in sight. She's wobbling slightly.

She looks like a tapeworm on legs.

11:24 a.m. She's making her way down the aisle toward Ned, the groom. He has a stunned expression on his face. Maybe he's having second thoughts about marrying someone who weighs about the same as a loaf of Wonder Bread.

11:25 The Eagle Has Landed. I repeat, the Eagle Has Landed. (That means the bride has reached the altar, to you civilians.)

11:26 a.m. Mumble mumble mumble. I can't hear a thing. Priest, bride, and groom all sound like they are talking with their faces pressed into a plate of mashed potatoes.

11:28 a.m. The cool girl is pulling out a pen and reaching for my notebook.

My name is Karma. What are you writing?

I'm Lily. I'm writing my memoirs so that when my biography is written, all the information will be in one easily accessible volume. Plus I get school credit.

Right—I get it. You're being a writer.

Yes.

I didn't think I was going to meet anyone interesting at this wedding. Those are my parents next to me, Veronique and Charles LeBlanc.

My parents are on the other side of me. They'll probably freak if they realize we're passing notes.

You should sit with us at the reception. Maybe we could actually have some fun that way.

Okay!

Ladies' room, the Geer Ballroom, DuPuis Hotel.

1:14 p.m. This all has to be planned meticulously. A brief scouting expedition has indicated the LeBlancs aren't inside the reception hall yet. But my parents ARE. I've made a quick check of the seating list—I'm supposed to be sitting at table fourteen with my parents and the Aunt Tiffy Show. The LeBlancs are assigned to table seventeen, and there are two empty spots.

Now, F.B.s, you and I both know that Lenny Blennerhassett Will Tolerate No Deviation from the Assigned Seating Charts!!! But if I time it just right, wait till the LeBlancs are sitting down, then slink in and sit down at their table in one smooth motion, the tables will be turned (no pun intended). (Actually, make it intentional.) Because once I'm sitting, my mother's sense of presenting a polite appearance will prevent her from coming over and making me get up and move. It's a watertight plan.

1:18 p.m. Hotel lobby adjacent to ballroom entrance. Position secure behind large leafy plant.

1:20 p.m. Close call with Uncle Ted, who just stubbed his cigar out in the planter.

1:22 p.m. LeBlancs sighted.

1:23 p.m. LeBlancs seated. I'M GOING IN!

1:25 p.m. Plan executed flawlessly. I am SITTING AT TABLE SEVENTEEN.

1:27 p.m. Mom has caught sight of me and is making the palm-inward-wag-fingers gesture that is the international parental gesture for "come here." I am waving back, pretending to mistake the "come here" gesture for the international "hey, how ya doing?" gesture.

1:28 p.m. Hushed tones at table fourteen.

1:29 p.m. No one is getting up from table fourteen. I am safe!

The Post-Game Report: A Little Table Seventeen Conversation as It Unfolded:

KARMA: Lily's a writer. She's writing down everything in a notebook so people in the future can study it. It's like reality TV, but for readers. Or something.

CHARLES: That's absolutely fascinating. Nothing is more important than recording the truth. This could be revolutionary, Lily. Don't you think, Veronique?

VERONIQUE: Extremely provocative.

ME: Yeah. Um, yes. That's my goal, of course. Revoke and provolutionize.

CHARLES: I can tell already you're going to be an extremely important person to your generation, Lily. Most of them can't get off the couch and put the Nintendo joystick down. I can't tell you how relieved I am to finally meet a young person other than my daughter who has a real spark in her. But you should be typing, not writing in a notebook. You've got to get yourself a laptop!

VERONIQUE: You see, Karma? I told you not to give up, and I was right. There is one interesting person here, and we've found her.

(Note: there are three other people at our table. There is Mr. Fisk, who is apparently Delia's personal trainer, powerfully muscled, totally bald, and looks like he might be a few fries short of a Happy Meal. There is a bodacious redhead who may or may not be Mrs. Fisk. And there is a huge, and I do mean huge, man with thick glasses and a big tuft of jet-black hair who has not identified himself or spoken at all.)

KARMA *(nudging me and gesturing toward Mr. Fisk, speaking in somewhat low voice)*: I'm betting he plays Tomb Raider and collects *Star Wars* dolls.

ME *(laughing behind hand)*: Definitely. What do you

think of the shaved head? The tough guy look, or dealing with a receding hairline?

KARMA *(grinning)*: Receding hairline, definitely. Follically challenged.

ME: I'm guessing his favorite band is Metallica.

KARMA: And hers is 'N'Sync.

ME: She collects Christmas-tree ornaments and ceramic angels.

KARMA: He leaves the toilet seat up after he pees.

VERONIQUE *(leaning toward us)*: She watches infomercials and buys hair-care products off cable-television shows.

ME *(trying not to look surprised that Veronique is playing)*: He wears the same shirt three days in a row and cries during Kodak commercials.

KARMA: The last book he read was *Weight Lifting for Dummies*.

ME: The last book she read was *Flaming Wings of Scottish Desire*.

VERONIQUE: *Part Two*.

(We all laugh. Suddenly Mr. Fisk stands up and glares at us. He is big. He is very, very big.)

MR. FISK: What do you think I am, deaf?

KARMA *(under her breath)*: Dumb.

MR. FISK: What was that? WHAT was that? You think I can't hear what you're saying?

CHARLES: Sit down. You're embarrassing yourself.

*(Mr. Fisk sits down, then gets partway up out of his
chair and leans toward us).*

MR. FISK: You think you can sit there and make fun of me
and Tina? What do you think you are, flipping royal
princesses?

*(Now Veronique stands up. She looks like some kind
of mod goddess. She's got really good posture, and buff
arms and a totally flat stomach. She gets this look of
outrage on her face, all by raising one finely plucked
eyebrow.)*

VERONIQUE: I don't think you have any idea what we were
talking about.

MR. FISK: Oh, I don't, don't I? 'Cause I think I do, lady,
and I don't stinking like it ONE BIT.

VERONIQUE: Ah, then you've read Principessa Di
Guadalupe's new essay collection?

MR. FISK *(looking confused)*: Eh?

VERONIQUE: Principessa Di Guadalupe's new collection of
essays.

CHARLES: *Wild Hill Clouds in Capri.* You look like a well-
read man, Mr. Fisk. Certainly you're familiar with Di
Guadalupe's work.

MR. FISK: Well . . . .

CHARLES: You see, Veronique? The man knows his Di
Guadalupe.

VERONIQUE: Then you'll recognize the stream-of-consciousness character exercises from her prologue that we are re-creating.

MR. FISK: Stream of . . . ?

CHARLES: You see, Veronique? He knows all about it.

VERONIQUE: Very good. Because for a moment I thought you were implying that we were speaking inappropriately, Mr. Fisk.

CHARLES: I believe you were mistaken, Veronique. Obviously the man recognizes a Di Guadalupe stream-of-consciousness exercise when he hears one.

VERONIQUE *(merrily)*: Well, they *are* hard to miss!

> *(Veronique and Charles laugh. Karma and I laugh.*
> *Mrs. Fisk, if that's who she is, giggles a little. Mr.*
> *Fisk looks around at all of us, then nods and sits back*
> *down.)*

MR. FISK: Yeah. Yeah, Guadalunchmeat. I know about all kinds of exercises, of course. That's my line of work. You name it, tae bo, yoga, Pilates, Nautilus . . .

KARMA : Di Guadalunchmeat . . .

MR. FISK: Exactly! Hey look, we got some food coming here! I'm starving.

> *(Veronique looks over at me and winks.)*

VERONIQUE: You're a vegetarian, aren't you, Lily?

ME: N—oh, I mean, absolutely. Absolutely!!

VERONIQUE: I knew you wouldn't disappoint. Make it four, Charles.

CHARLES: Four vegetarian meals, please.

WAITER: Well, I'm not sure . . . that is, was this set up in advance? Because I don't believe the caterer received those instructions—

CHARLES: They're dreadful, aren't they, caterers. High-strung and completely unreliable. I bet they make your life a living hell.

WAITER: Well, that's true. This one is especially bad.

CHARLES: Look, I'm certainly going to make a complaint about the lack of communication in the kitchen. The caterer will catch a lot of grief, you can count on it. And of course we'll make a special point of explaining how helpful you were *(reading waiter's name tag)*, Tim. Unfortunately, in the meantime, my girls are getting hungry.

TIM THE WAITER: I'll work something out, sir. I'll get something for you on the double.

CHARLES *(smiling and looking resplendent)*: I appreciate it, Tim.

(Tim leaves, bearing grin of pride and honor.)

VERONIQUE: Well, Lily, we haven't seen your folks in about ten years. Lenny's an accountant, isn't he?

ME: Yes.

CHARLES: That's all right, no need to apologize! We all need folks who know how to crunch those numbers. Not everyone can do the exciting work. Does pretty well, does he?

ME: Oh, sure, he does really well. Great! I mean, we're not

walking around on mink carpets or anything—

KARMA: God forbid! Are people killing animals now to make carpets out of them, too? Coats aren't bad enough?

VERONIQUE: Karma, Lily is JOKING! Aren't you, Lily, sweets?

ME: Oh, of course! I mean. Gosh! Yes! I just meant, you know, that we weren't like Bill Gates rich or something. But yeah, Dad does really well. We live in a pretty nice area, and we have the lake house and everything.

CHARLES: Lake house?

It was then that somebody, the master of ceremonies or something, got behind the mike and informed us that Delia and Ned would be having their first dance. I glanced over to table fourteen to see how things were going. The hushed tones appeared to have fallen by the wayside. My father was just returning from the bar with two radioactive-looking beverages. I've seen them before. They're called gimlets. Each gimlet, once you drink it, apparently creates the desire for additional gimlets. Sort of like Edmund and the Turkish delight in *The Lion, the Witch and the Wardrobe,* which I certainly hope, Future Biographers, that you have read.

The food had all been eaten and removed. Delia and Ned did the old cut-the-wedding-cake-and-feed-it-to-each-other trick (except Delia didn't actually swallow her bite). I've got to say, it was pretty lame, even though I was sitting at the Cool Table.

After the cake cutting, the LeBlancs took off. Just like that. Veronique was asking me about the public schools in my neighborhood, and I told her I went to private school. Then Charles said something to her, and they all got up and said they'd see me later.

Then I saw my mother was making the "come here" gesture. I didn't have the strength to make conversation with the Fisks or Silent Man, so I gave in and went over. I received a very long lecture with many questions for which there were few answers. Why did I not proceed to table fourteen, as the seating chart very clearly indicated (that one from Dad)? Why did I feel it acceptable to sit apart from my immediate family, and how did I think that looked to others (that one from Mom)?

And then, F.B.s, my mother told me I should not have sat with the LeBlancs. She said they were "not the right people" for me.

Not the right people, F.B.s? For me? Is it not enough that my parents keep me from everything interesting, loud, frosted, or exceeding 55 miles per hour? Is it not enough that my home life has the ability to bore a person senseless? Is it not enough that I am effectively being kept from any and all experiences that I might possibly draw upon in the creation of my first novel? Are all these things not enough? Or must I also be told that the only interesting and different people I have met for weeks, for months, FOR YEARS, are NOT THE RIGHT PEOPLE FOR ME?

I'm going to take a nap.

9:07 p.m. Life is brightening! The Blennerhassetts had a light and sadly tasteless dinner in the hotel restaurant, then the parentals went out for a quick walk (my father calls them constitutionals). And I spotted Charles and Veronique in the lobby! Veronique saw me, and she beckoned me over and gave me a hug (!!). She had a mischievous look on her face, and she asked me if I was up for a midnight swim.

Social stupidity is a learned behavior, and I've simply had too much practice at home to unlearn it all at once. So I heard myself, as if from a great distance, say, "But doesn't the pool close at ten?" And Charles pointed his finger at me (with what I like to consider was stern affection) and said, "They can't legislate water." And I found myself nodding. Just like that.

I think you'll agree, F.B.s, that it is in the best interest of all parties concerned if I neglect to inform Lenny and Phyllis of this plan.

Hotel room.

11:38 p.m. I should look into some sort of gimlet home-delivery service, because those things really knocked my parents out. Like I said, we have a suite with two bedrooms, and they are sacked out in theirs, snoring blissfully, unaware that their daughter has just slipped into a bathing suit and fat terry-cloth robe.

Look, F.B.s, just between you and me and the Future Literature Students of America, I'm a little nervous about stealing out at midnight in my bathrobe.

11:49 p.m. I'm going.

11:51 p.m. I'm not going.

11:55 p.m. Should I go?

11:57 p.m. It's now or never.

*Hotel room. **This is my story, and I'm sticking to it.***

Time Unknown. The LeBlancs were already at the pool when I got there. I had been taking great pains to move quietly (the word "stealth" should appear somewhere in this sentence—perhaps my Future Editor will find the right spot?), but Karma and her parents were laughing and chattering and carrying on like it was the middle of the day.

The pool looked kind of unreal in the dark. Like it was a very accurate reproduction of a pool, but not something a person was meant to be jumping into. You'll think I'm crazy, F.B.s, but that pool had a challenging look to it. Like it didn't really expect me to plunge in.

"You first," Karma said.

My lame response: "It's awfully dark in there."

Well, it WAS awfully dark in there. And there is something very creepy about getting into the water when you can't see the bottom of the pool. I mean, were we absolutely certain that the hotel manager didn't use the pool at night to exercise his pet great white shark?

Charles said I must be used to swimming in the lake by our lake house. He asked if we went there a lot. I told him we always went for two weeks every August, and that I did swim in the lake every day, but never at night. He asked if we rented the house out for the rest of the year, and I said not anymore.

That was when Veronique walked over to the lifeguard station and flicked on a switch. And suddenly the whole area was flooded with light. I couldn't help making a little startled noise. Stealth was no longer in the running. Then all of them seemed to be looking at me at once—Karma in her shimmery bikini, Veronique with her dark hair piled high, looking sleek in a blue one-piece, and Charles, inexplicably, in khakis and a button-down.

It was a life moment, F.B.s. It was Robert Frost's two roads diverging in the wood. It was time to choose sides, Blennerhassett Circle or LeBlanc Boulevard. Time to make a statement about who I had been up until now, and who I wanted to be in the future. It was time to reach out and grab experience by the horns, like every writer must.

I took the plunge.

The rest, as they say, is history. Shortly after I jumped into the pool, a bellboy appeared on the scene. A bellboy with a giant chip on his shoulder, a bellboy who obviously so resented every carbon life form on two legs who had ever checked into the DuPuis Hotel that —I COMPLETELY lost my train of thought. Charles is right, I need a laptop.

We were ordered out of the pool area. The LeBlancs just laughed it off. They seemed to think the whole thing was hysterical, and it was. It should have been. But I was the one being escorted back to my room by the assistant night manager. I was the one who was going to have to face parents awakened from a gimlet-induced slumber, while Karma and HER parents giggled their way up to their room, their arms around one another.

It isn't fair.

Sunday, June 30
The Blennerhassett residence.

As if I care that I'm grounded for five days. As if I have anywhere go to ANYWAY. As if it matters that my last creative impulses are being smothered. DID EMILY DICKINSON'S PARENTS EVER GROUND HER?

Monday, July 1
Szechuan House.

6:00 p.m. I'm on furlough. That, F.B.s, is a very good word for a brief leave of absence granted to a soldier or prisoner. I like to think of myself as a bit of both. Anyway, I'm on furlough because it's my father's birthday, and he's a guy who likes to do things the way they've always been done. That's why we're at Szechuan House for his birthday dinner. In approximately four minutes, my father will order us two Peking ducks, just like he did last year and the year before. He will also order the pupu platter for three, and my mother will giggle. When it arrives, and only one fried wonton is left, my father will point to it and say, "There's only one ton left!" When the two ducks arrive, he will point to their combined leg count of four and ask the waiter if he has accidentally brought us Peking dog. We will all be required to use chopsticks. Dad will ask the waiter to take away the forks, and he'll say, "When in Rome!" Then he'll wink.

My life is a rerun. At least they're letting me write at the table (more furlough, I guess), so F.B.s may understand why Lily Blennerhassett requested that no duck be served at her National Book Award dinner.

6:04 p.m. Pupu platter and two Peking ducks just ordered. All forks removed from table. Wink complete.

There is a man sitting alone at a table, eating dumplings and staring thoughtfully at the restaurant's aquarium. If Karma and her parents were here, we'd probably be guessing what his job was, and why he was eating alone, and how his last girlfriend broke up with him. Maybe he's thinking about liberating the lobsters in the tank. I'm sure the LeBlancs would approve of crustacean liberation. If he makes a move, I'm ready to provide backup.

6:22 p.m. Only one ton left. My mother eats it.

6:38 p.m. Peking dog joke receives feeble laugh. Lobsters still incarcerated. My mother is saying, "Lily, for heaven's sake, will you put that diary down and eat your dinner!" I am powerless in the face of this censorship.

7:10 p.m. Fortune cookies and fried bananas have been consumed. When the waiter gives Dad the bill, he will put on his Groucho Marx accent and say, "This is an outrage. If I were you, I wouldn't pay it." The waiter will smile and nod and probably contemplate employment elsewhere.

7:15 p.m. No Groucho joke. How can Dad have let that happen? Is he distracted? And the man in the corner has paid his bill and left without freeing the lobsters. Is there any hope for my writer's life?

Tuesday, July 2

My life is bleaker than an orphan in a Roald Dahl novel. There's nothing like being told you can't go anywhere to make a person who otherwise wouldn't want to go anywhere want to go somewhere. (Future Editor, see what you can do with that sentence, okay?)

Lenny spilled carrot juice on his shirt just before leaving for work this morning, throwing the entire household into an upheaval. And Phyllis is irritated because the phone keeps ringing, and when she answers, no one is on the other end. And as you know, I am imprisoned high in the tower of my bedroom, the Rapunzel of the literary world, scribbling away because certain immediate ancestors have never even considered buying me a laptop computer.

I bet Karma and Veronique go to the gym and do kickboxing together. Or attend Pilates classes. Or take weeks at the spa. The girl really is perfect, and I say that with NO resentment in my heart. She looks like some hip, sophisticated, but all-natural version of Cher. Karma should be an action figure, a Saturday-morning cartoon, a breakfast cereal. There should be Karma Societies and Karma websites. She is the culmination of the American dream. And I am not.

The killer part of it all is Karma actually seems to *like* me. As in wants-to-be-friends kind of likes. Friends with *me*, the poster child for imperfection and boringness. Just hanging around someone like that could do wonders for my creative base, not to mention my self-esteem. But my parents whisked me out of the DuPuis Hotel three hours before checkout time. They followed me around like Elmer Fudd stalking Bugs Bunny. I never had a chance to say good-bye to the LeBlancs, or get their number. And they're not in the book. I checked.

Wednesday, July 3
Still home.

All I have left is *Star Trek*. I glean tiny drops of comfort (is that good, Future Editors? I think it sounds kind of snappy) from Captains Kirk, Sisko, Picard, and (my favorite) Janeway. Oh, the things I could do as Captain Lily Blennerhassett-Janeway, my hair piled high in a bun, my voice clipped, my starship crew fulfilling my every command.

I'm allowed to watch television while grounded, F.B.s, because my parents know I don't really like it all that much. Let's just keep the *Star Trek* thing between us, okay?

More phone calls with no one there today. Phyllis is talking about changing our phone number to an unlisted one. As if.

2:50 p.m. Have been trying to reach Charlotte since breakfast! What kind of Young Executive training is she receiving if I can't even get a message through to her? This is INFURIATING!

2:55 p.m. I am not at all jealous that Charlotte is so busy. I can choose exactly what I want to do, when I want to do it. If an idea comes into my head, I can go with it. No problem. No planned activities, no schedule, no meetings. I'm the master of my fate. The choreographer of my day. The architect of my world.

I'm going to reorganize all my books in alphabetical order.

2:58 p.m. Apparently my books are already in alphabetical order.

3:40 p.m. Reorganized contents of refrigerator, paired off condiment bottles by size with subsection for spicy or imported sauces. Cleaned the top of the milk and orange juice cartons and Mom's Diet Barq's root beer six-pack, which was really quite grubby. Pried a small piece of dried, flattened broccoli off the inside of the vegetable drawer.

What would have happened if I had not been home and able to see to this?

4:20 Why not start a short story? It's quiet, and I have the time. I'm going for it!

It was the summer of my thirteenth year when I stumbled upon the shocking truth. It

5:00 p.m. I'm blocked. I can't write any more fiction today.

TEN PEOPLE DOLPHINS ARE SMARTER THAN:
1) Enrique Iglesias
2) Danielle Steele
3) Prince Charles
4) Madame Daspis (last year's French teacher)
5) Pamela Anderson's next husband

6) Melissa Rivers

7) Barbie

8) Any professional wrestler

9) Christina Aguilera

10) The Pet Psychic from Animal Planet

It's important to record these insights as they are received.

7:01 p.m. I would hate to become the first person in recorded history to ACTUALLY DIE OF BOREDOM!!

8:48 p.m. Contemplating changing my handwriting. Candidates:

Lily Blennerhassett

Lily Blennerhassett

Lily Blennerhassett

Lily Blennerhassett

Lily Blennerhassett

11:03 p.m. I wonder what Karma is doing. Probably something sophisticated. Probably something classy, and unusual, and fat free. Probably not sitting around wondering what I am doing.

How long would it take me to grow my hair out like hers?

Thursday, July 4
The kitchen.

9:00 a.m. This is the first good thing to happen to me since Delia's reception. After a lengthy conversation in hushed tones, Lenny and Phyllis gravely informed me that it was their decision that my grounding should not be lifted in order for me to attend the annual Fourth of July picnic hosted by the Daughters of the American Revolution on the village green. That I should instead remain home with my thoughts and contemplate my behavior.

Yeeee-hah!

9:45 a.m. I'm going to go for a nice, vigorous, and mind-expanding hike.

SUPPLY CHECKLIST:
Water bottle (primary)
Water bottle (spare)
Sunblock
Protein bar (chocolate)
Protein bar (banana)
Protein bar (wild berry)
Insect repellent
Band-Aids (in case of blister)
Extra socks
Hat with visor

Sunglasses

Pocket reptile guide (to evaluate if snakes poisonous)

10:02 a.m. I'm going!

10:17 a.m. It was hot out there. And bright. And buggy. But I think I got a decent workout. I really do. And one protein bar STILL UNEATEN!

10:40 a.m. Called Charlotte, no answer.

10:50 a.m. Called Charlotte, no answer.

10:58 a.m. Called Charlotte, line busy!

11:03 a.m. Called Charlotte, no answer. How can she do this to me?

11:54 a.m. My hair doesn't seem to look at all different, and I've been growing it out now for almost 24 hours.

Telphn rngng mght b chrlott!!!

12:07 p.m. Future Biographers. FUTURE BIOGRA-PHERS! You will NEVER guess who that was on the phone!! But you can spend hours looking it up in the Blennerhassett Literary Archives, so I'll save you the trouble. It was Karma! Imagine the luck of that, the one time I answer the phone in days, and it is Karma!

And here is the really wild part—she and her parents are in the neighborhood, and they are STOPPING BY!

I have to admit, I'm a little nervous about it. Lenny and Phyllis always stay through the very end of the Living Revolution Historical Re-creation that the Daughters of the

American Revolution stage on the green. But there is the possibility something could go wrong, and they could come home unexpectedly. However, risk makes the writer! I am ready to start living on the edge. What—

Are they here already?

2:00 p.m. Whoa. That was . . . they were so . . . I mean, first they pulled up in this amazing slinky silver car, which had an Italian name that I can't remember. Karma had done her hair in hundreds of teeny braids and she was wearing denim capri pants with hand-painted dragons on the sides. Charles looked fresh but casual, like the president looks when he's photographed on holiday. And Veronique had this incredible halter-top dress in a tiny purple paisley pattern. I wanted to change my clothes when I saw them get out of the car, but everything I have is just as stupid looking as what I was already wearing. They didn't seem to notice or they were too polite to say anything—anyway they came inside and they ALL hugged me and they were soooooooooo nice.

My Visit with the Cool People:

CHARLES: Lily! You're too modest! This is a really lovely home.
ME: Oh. Thank you.

CHARLES: I'm all for understated decor myself.

VERONIQUE: It's less cluttered that way.

KARMA: Less ostentatious.

CHARLES AND VERONIQUE: Exactly.

> *(I provide the house tour. We end up back in the kitchen. I offer coffee, but they don't drink caffeine. They ask for green tea, but we don't have any. So they settle for hot water with lemon. Veronique says it is a very ancient and healthful tonic.)*

KARMA: Lily, I can't believe you got in trouble because of us. That really rots. (*To her parents*) Lily is grounded for five days!

CHARLES. No! You ARE joking, Karma?

ME: It's true, I'm afraid. My parents weren't too happy I broke hotel rules by going swimming.

VERONIQUE: They punished you for going swimming? In a public swimming pool? That sounds a little severe.

> *(It DOES sound a little severe, now that she mentions it.)*

I mean, it's not as if she stole a car.

CHARLES: Well now, Veronique, not everyone parents as we do. I'm sure Lily's mother and father felt as if they were acting in her best interests.

ME (*in subject-changing mode*): I love your watch, Veronique.

VERONIQUE: Oh, aren't you sweet, and what a good eye

you have! It's titanium. The new gold.

(I nod wisely, pouring hot water over little slices of lemon for everyone.)

CHARLES: Still, I think it's rather un-American to leave you here alone on the Fourth of July. Independence Day is family day, after all.

KARMA *(putting an arm around me)*: Well, WE'RE Lily's family, too!

VERONIQUE: Yes, of course we are! You're an honorary LeBlanc, Lily.

(I glow.)

CHARLES: Is your father back in the office tomorrow?

ME: Yes. He just gets the one day off.

CHARLES: And what about your mother?

ME: Oh, she doesn't work. I mean, she takes lots of classes, and does volunteer work and things, but she doesn't have a job job.

VERONIQUE: Well, that's nothing to be ashamed of! What are decades of women's rights good for, anyway, unless a woman can take advantage of the CHOICE to not personally participate in her newly elevated position in society? I think that's wonderful. Really, I do. I fully, completely support that. Really.

(Veronique's nails are perfect. They are just long enough to look classy and not tacky. They are a glossy crimson. Her fingers are like little works of art, real

long and slender. I can't stop looking at them.)

KARMA: And I don't agree that it makes other women look bad.

VERONIQUE: Of course it doesn't!

(I nod, and nod, and nod. I don't know who Karma is disagreeing with, but I'm sure she only means to be nice, and I nod some more.)

CHARLES: And it is extremely empowering to Lily to have her mother here full-time, to benefit from that influence. I sometimes think you might have been better off with a little more Veronique and a little less nanny, Karma.

(Karma shrugs and tosses her hair. How could she have been different with her mother around more? She already seems to have turned out perfectly.)

VERONIQUE: Oh, Lily, I am so, so glad we've met you!

KARMA: We almost didn't go to the wedding at all. Veronique and Charles don't approve of lavish weddings.

VERONIQUE *(very seriously)*: It's not that we don't wish Ned and Delia the very best. But we do feel that weddings in this society have reached outlandish and unnecessary proportions. Delia's dress alone probably cost five thousand dollars, and she'll wear it only once! There are plenty of people in the world who could use the fifteen or twenty thousand dollars they spent on that wedding to buy food and clothes for an entire year.

KARMA: The waste was unbelievable! Flowers, candles,

decorations. It all went in the trash the next day. They could have taken all that money, minus a hundred and fifty bucks for the marriage license and some chips, and done some real good in the world!

(I'm suddenly totally understanding what they're saying. That wedding was outlandish! Criminal, practically! How did I not see it before?)

ME: You are so right! I felt the exact same way for the whole wedding. What are people thinking when they drop that kind of money on a silly party?

VERONIQUE: They do it because it's all about appearances, about impressing other people. Creating a false front. A pretense.

KARMA: A show-off.

VERONIQUE: Precisely.

CHARLES *(sitting back in the kitchen chair and stretching his legs out—he looks absolutely presidential, but in a caring, really enlightened way)*: Well, we've done our little part to correct their mistake, anyway. Delia and Ned were registered for wedding gifts at Lovely Homes. You should have seen the list of flashy and unnecessary items on their wish list. But we didn't buy them a wedding gift there. Instead, we gave them a letter telling them we will be making a donation to the Red Cross in their name. In thirty years, when all the crystal glasses and cappuccino makers and other material possessions they were given are broken and useless, Ned and Delia will at least have some comfort in the fact that, because we refused to indulge in the nuptial materialism, they unwittingly did some good in the world.

(Oh F.B.s! Don't these people ROCK?!!)

Pretty soon after that, they had to go. I think there was somewhere else they had to be. I feel so uplifted, so transformed! I'm glad I let Karma see my room. She was right—the Britney Spears dartboard was beneath me and had to go, and why did I need that fake polar bearskin rug by my bed? Karma did me a favor by putting it in the garbage herself. The LeBlancs all seem to have this talent for knowing what looks good. And the best thing is I'm going to see them again! Apparently Charles and Veronique have founded an environmental watchdog program called Hug the Planet. The office is right in town, on Main Street. Karma is helping out with work there, and they said I can stop by whenever I feel like it.

Charles explained that no matter how misguided we knew my parents were, it was important to be respectful of their feelings, even the negative ones they seemed strangely to have about the LeBlancs. He said I could do that by having understanding in my heart for their misguided protectiveness and to know that it was love for me that made them act in such a confused and inappropriate way over the swimming incident. But Charles also said I could be respectful to myself and my own needs by simply finding ways to visit Karma without letting my parents know and unnecessarily upsetting them. In this way, everyone's needs are fulfilled.

THIS is effective parenting! THESE are the empathetic, with-it parents that generations of children have prayed for! FINALLY! Charles LeBlanc is the Dalai Lama of fathers!

8:45 p.m. Still unable to get Charlotte, and you'll notice, F.B.s, that SHE has not called me. Just as well. If I had reached her today, I might have yakked for an hour and the phone would have been busy when Karma called and I would never have known they were passing through my neighborhood. So Charlotte did me a favor. And that's all I have to say about it.

Saturday, July 6
Backseat of Honda.

I'd give just about anything to be grounded again. Lenny and Phyllis are celebrating the end of my grounding by taking me on an F.O. to the newly opened Lewis County Quilt Museum. Clearly they are bent on destroying my newfound will to live. Thirty minutes in the backseat while we clog the fast lane on the interstate, and the Honda's air conditioning is failing.

Still, I'm doing as Charles suggested. When they told me my grounding was over and they hoped we all now had an understanding about the LeBlancs, I just nodded and said I totally understood where they were coming from, and that I wouldn't make the same mistake again. (What I really meant was I totally understood how bogus and misguided they were, and I would never again make the mistake of hanging around the LeBlancs where they could catch me. That Charles, he is some kind of genius in addition to being a real snappy dresser).

The tour director known only as "Mom" has announced that we have arrived and the time has come to plumb the mysterious depths of the world of quilts. This looks bad. I'm pretty certain there is no decent snack bar inside.

Phyllis is threatening to wrestle my diary from my hands unless I get out of the car. She

Monday, July 8

How could I have forgotten? Phyllis has jury duty this week! No F.O.s, no constant surveillance. I can visit Hug the Planet. Maybe stuff some envelopes or something, and share a pot of green tea with the LeBlancs! Have a chat! Oh, happy, happy day. I could even go right now!

But what will I wear? And what about my hair? It's a really bad length right now. Maybe I could try that braid thing Karma did.

Phone's ringing.

Faithful Rendition of Phone Conversation:

CHARLOTTE: Hi, it's me!

ME: Charlotte? Where have you been?

CHARLOTTE: What do you mean, where have I been? I've been here—at camp.

ME: I've tried to get you about a million times, and no one ever answers.

CHARLOTTE: I'm sorry. It's just that we're hardly ever in our rooms.

ME: You could have called me. It was your turn.

CHARLOTTE: We can't make outgoing calls on the phones in our rooms, except to our parents. I'm on the pay phone behind the dining hall—it's finally free. I'm sorry, Lily—are you mad at me? Don't be mad at me. It's bad enough being here without you.

ME *(melting suddenly)*: I'm not mad. Do I sound mad? Do you really miss me?

CHARLOTTE: I totally miss you. I think I've gotten all I can out of Young Executive Camp. But it's paid for, so I have to stay till the end. Are you as bored as I am?

ME: Yes and no. I mean, I was bored because I was grounded for five days. But now I'm free again.

CHARLOTTE: You got grounded? Why? It's been years since you've been grounded.

ME: Well, actually, I met this really cool girl at Delia's wedding, and we snuck into the pool at midnight for a swim. And we got caught.

CHARLOTTE: Why? What were you thinking? You snuck into the pool? You're too old to do stuff like that, Lily.

ME *(a bit defensive)*: Well, it was the girl's PARENTS' idea, actually.

CHARLOTTE: Must be pretty dumb parents.

ME *(indignant)*: On the contrary! Veronique and Charles happen to be widely respected environmental activists, not to mention extremely modern and understanding parents. Unlike my own, who totally wigged out when we got caught. Dad went on and on about trust violation and how nobody is above the rules, no matter what we think of them, and what would happen if everyone stopped following the rules they thought were dumb, and blah blah blah.

CHARLOTTE: Your father is an intelligent and very sensible citizen.

ME: He is a doofus. Both my parents are.

CHARLOTTE: They were right to be mad at you. And you say this girl's PARENTS were along too? Encouraging you to break the hotel rules? That's ridiculous. They might as well have given you beer and cigarettes, too.

ME: They are totally superior.

CHARLOTTE: I don't thiiiiiink sooooo. . . .

ME *(reverting to age 8)*: They are.

CHARLOTTE: Not.

ME *(reverting to age 6)*: Are! Are!

CHARLOTTE: This is stupid. Let's talk about something else.

ME *(resisting the urge to keep arguing on the LeBlancs' behalf until Charlotte UNDERSTANDS how cool they are)*: You're right. You'll have to meet them to realize how great they are. So when are you coming back?

CHARLOTTE: July 19, remember? Don't you have a Palm Pilot? A date book at least? An organizer? Filofax?

ME: July 19—that's FOREVER! Can you sleep over the night you get home?

CHARLOTTE: I don't know. I'll start working on Mom. If not, then the next night. Tacos and root beer.

ME: Yay! How's your Think Tank Boy Partner?

CHARLOTTE: He got expelled.

ME: What? Expelled from camp?

CHARLOTTE: He broke into another team's lab room and sabotaged the hard drives on all their laptops to give our team the advantage, without my knowledge, of course, then he tripped the fire alarm on the way out to create a diversion.

ME: I can't believe it. You're now telling me that you have boys, scandals, AND laptops at Young Executive Camp? Maybe I was wrong about it.

CHARLOTTE: Now you say so. When it's too late to sign up. Oh, I'm going to be late for my Think Tank brainstorm session!

ME: Okay, go, go. Try and get expelled or something so you can come home sooner.

CHARLOTTE: I'm sorry we had to go separate ways this summer. If I'd stayed home, maybe I could have gone to that wedding and stopped that girl and her criminal parents from getting you in trouble.

ME *(feeling surprisingly irritated at the way Charlotte is talking about the LeBlancs)*: Okay, later.

CHARLOTTE: 'Bye.

   (Endus conversationus.)

11:55 a.m. I have to wait until after lunch to go visit Hug the Planet, on the off chance my mother comes home for lunch. That gives me one hour and five minutes to kill.

Brief Daydreaming Interlude:

1) Stow away on a freighter crossing the Atlantic Ocean. Discover mutiny plot via eavesdropping, foil plot. Win Congressional Medal of Honor. Karma sees me on television and sends flowers.

2) Save president from attack dogs using only a raincoat and a coat hanger as weapons. Win Congressional Medal of Honor. LeBlancs attend ceremony.

3) Pass burning house, call 911 on cell phone while simultaneously dragging all occupants, including pets, to safety. Win Congressional Medal of Honor. Saved occupants happen to be Karma and her parents, who express their gratitude by taking me to their palatial vacation home in Bora Bora, and eventually legally adopting me into their family.

4) Unwittingly discover cure for cancer by combining organic fruit juices with baking soda. Give secret formula to the government for free. Win Congressional Medal of Honor. Formula used to save life of LeBlancs' aged and dearly loved great-aunt. When great-aunt drinks cure and gets out of wheelchair after five years of paralysis, Charles and Veronique weep and Karma has my name tattooed on her arm as a gesture of thanks.

5) Save Karma from crazed stalking admirer who is obsessed with obtaining a lock of her hair. Deliver crazed admirer into the hands of the FBI. Look humble as Karma tells me that because of my brave actions, she can now live her life without fear.

1:10 p.m. I'm going to Hug the Planet! I'm not taking my notebook, though. It just seems a little dorky to be carrying it with me all the time. I don't want Karma to think I'm some kind of squidget brain.

Sometime After Dinner. Karma and I are TOTALLY FATED to be friends. I was walking down Main Street toward the address I had for Hug the Planet, and I ran into Karma right on the sidewalk! She said Charles and Veronique were having this really important meeting back at the office with some government high-up (whose name she's not even allowed to tell me—wow!) so we went over to the Tea Leaf together and had chai lattes.

We talked and talked. She told me about her last boyfriend, who she met in Switzerland, but he is actually an exiled Italian count who's being kept from his castle and his riches by his stepmother, who is related to the king of Greece or one of those places. And then she asked me a lot of questions about my parents, and she told me she thought it was really brutally unfair that my mother didn't let me pick out my own clothes. (I didn't even tell her that—she just knew!) And she said Veronique had always believed that a child's right to choose her own outfits was one of the cornerstones of good parenting, because it is the first step a person takes toward knowing and expressing her Inner Self. And I told her that to be honest I had been wearing clothes my mother picked out for so long, I wouldn't know a good outfit if it bit me. So THEN—Karma offered to go shopping with me and BE MY FASHION ADVISOR!!!

I'm really only supposed to use my American Express card for emergencies. My parents gave it to me in case I ever got stranded somewhere, or for some reason needed access to money. But they never specifically said fashion emergencies didn't count. And actually, I'd had the card for two years now and never used it even once! So in a way, it seemed the card kind of owed me a few. And Karma was so psyched to get me into some new clothes. It wasn't as if I had a choice!

And this place Karma took me, Fioluzzi, I've never even seen before! It must have some kind of Trendy Cloaking Device around it—regular people can walk by and never see it. Karma took me in and made a beeline for these incredible pants that looked like the sky—light blue with dyed white splotches that looked like clouds. And they were only $81, which Karma said was practically HALF what they were worth. I tried them on with this white tank top Karma handed me, then looked in the mirror. Except for my hair, I hardly recognized myself! Then Karma came up behind me with this iridescent hair clip, and she scooped my hair up and put the clip in and suddenly . . . I was cool. There I was in the mirror, and I was cool.

Karma said there was no sense spending money on a great outfit and then neglecting shoes and accessories. Pointy slingback sandals, dangly silver earrings, an anklet, and a wrist cuff. It was the new me! I was gathering all my purchases together when I noticed Karma looking at this beaded shirt in different Indian patterns. She said it was just her luck—she'd been waiting for them to get this shirt in her size, but naturally she didn't have her credit card on her. It was really no big deal for me to add it to my stuff. After what she'd done for me I was totally thrilled to get it for her. I know she would do the same for me. And it was a very reasonable $96, a real steal for all that hand beading, Karma said.

Oh, F.B.s, it was the best, best day. It was like Karma reinvented me. I have never felt so hip before. When it was time to go, I rushed home and hid my clothes under the bed. At the appropriate time I'll sneak the items into my daily wardrobe. Maybe my mother won't notice.

And really, $367 isn't all that much, right?

Tuesday, July 9
The Blennerhassett living room.

My mother has returned from jury duty all giddy from her brush with our legal system. She's met some idiot dental assistant she wants to fix up with her (divorced) older brother, Mick. Phyllis's doomed fix-ups are legendary. The last time she set up this particular brother with a date, it was with a hair-color consultant who Phyllis swore shared Mick's passion for *Madame Butterfly* and *Don Giovanni*. Turns out there was a slight misunderstanding—the woman was an Oprah fanatic, not an opera fanatic. I don't think the date lasted past eight.

I would like to truly and sincerely thank the persons or institutions responsible for the disappearance in this country of the tradition whereby parents arrange their children's marriages.

Wednesday, July 10

9:30 a.m. Phyllis off to jury duty, and Lenny safely at work. I've got my new outfit on, top to bottom. I am COOL. Time to visit Hug the Planet! Whoopee! Will write about it when I get home—MUST stop lugging dumb notebook everywhere—it is not a cool accessory.

Later. The office was really small and simple. I'll privately admit, F.B.s, I was a little surprised by that at first. It's just two little rooms with a couple of cots and a small window and a tiny bathroom. But then Karma explained that Charles and Veronique refuse to get anything fancier, because they want all the money donated to HTP to go to important programs, like stopping whales and trees from being damaged and things. She showed me some leaflets about it, which she said I could keep. It's a lot of work getting the information together and getting it out to the public, and making them listen. The cots are so that employees working late nights doing mailings can take a nap. They just can't afford to put in foldout couches or anything. Karma said Charles couldn't live with himself if he spent one penny more than he had to on their own offices when the money could be going somewhere it was desperately needed. I just think that is so noble. I'll bet you don't see the Red Cross and the Salvation Army in tiny plain offices!

Karma is not even getting paid for her work at HTP. She probably wants the money to go to the whales and trees, just like Charles's would-be office rent money that he's not putting out for a fancier place. I need to try and be more like this—to think about the Greater Good before considering my own very small and insignificant needs. What am I really doing for the world? Writing everything down in a notebook? Is that going to help anyone?

I'm just realizing now how incredibly closed my life has been—I mean, I knew I lived a boring and uninteresting existence, but now I know HOW boring. Karma helped me see that I've really been imprisoned in Lenny and Phyllis's little world of speed limits and F.O.s when there is so much to be done in the world and so many experiences a person can have and animals that need to be protected and money that can be diverted from two-bedroom duplexes to actual trees that have been standing for two thousand years but are helpless in the path of loggers that— Oh, I've been SWEPT AWAY by this sentence. And because I have to write everything in longhand because I DON'T HAVE A LAPTOP, I'm stuck with my first draft forever. I apologize, Future Editors. The blame's with L & P. And with me. Karma says I should write less, and *do* more. She's right.

The visit ended around lunchtime, and Charles and Veronique asked Karma and me to go pick up some food so we could have a picnic lunch. Karma took me to this organic gourmet food shop called LaBouche & Garibaldi. Of course, trust me to act stupid in spite of my happening outfit—the first thing I saw that I thought looked good was hickory-cured turkey breast with a pesto glaze. Karma gave me this look, which I totally deserved, and said, "We're vegetarians, remember? I thought you were one, too." And my face was bright red and I said something totally idiotic like "Oh, I am. I just forget sometimes." So Karma said, "Maybe you should write it down in your little book so you remember." I knew my notebook was doofus-y. What a relief I didn't bring it with me! From now on I'm only going to write when I'm alone. I made enough of a fool of myself already.

Karma ordered for us. She is really sophisticated, and she ordered this incredible stuff. Squash blossoms stuffed with eggplant caviar. White truffle and cucumber sandwiches. Two pints of nettle soup, a quart of wild morel and porcini mushroom salad, a pound of Puget Beauty strawberries, and two pints of rose-petal ice cream.

You'd think they'd have been a little nicer seeing as we were buying all that stuff. But when Karma's credit card got rejected, the guy behind the counter was positively icy. It wasn't like it was Karma's *fault*—she was using the Hug the Planet corporate card, which apparently was temporarily maxed out after the purchase of three inflatable motorboats for the volunteers going out to stop whale hunters. Here there are people risking their lives navigating these little boats between the whales and the harpoons to stop the killing, and somebody has to pay for those boats—couldn't the guy behind the counter at least act a little grateful that someone was making the sacrifice because he was too busy selling wild morels and porcini mushrooms to do his part? But he just har-rumphed. So naturally I handed over my American Express card. It was the least I could do. And maybe it would make up for the roast turkey nightmare. So the guy took my card, but he still acted prissy about it, which I found hard to believe considering we'd just spent $103 buying our lunch from him.

The Picnic Interlude:

CHARLES: That's it right there—a perfect spot by the lake.

VERONIQUE: It looks as if it were made for a picnic.

ME (*genetically incapable of stifling stupid remarks*): Oh . . . but . . . doesn't that sign say KEEP OUT, PRIVATE PROPERTY?

CHARLES: Lily, Lily, Lily. You don't really subscribe to that, do you?

ME: No . . . to what?

CHARLES: Ownership of land? I don't acknowledge the concept. Remember what Chief Seattle said: "How can you buy the sky?"

ME: No, totally! I just . . . of course. Yes.

VERONIQUE: Let's go, then.

(So I follow them, and simply choose not to mention the other sign. The one that said GUARD DOG AND SECURITY PATROL ON DUTY. Hadn't I displayed enough ignorance and stupidity for one day?)

CHARLES: Here we are. Let's get this spread out, and tuck in!

VERONIQUE: Well, this all looks delicious, doesn't it? LaBouche & Garibaldi, I presume?

KARMA: Of course. It's the only decent place in town. I don't understand why there isn't a better selection of fresh, high-quality imported organic food here. Why is everyone so complacent and content to eat their disgusting hamburgers and tacos morning, noon, and night? Little greasy bites of capitalism, that's all they are.

CHARLES: Not everyone has had the advantages you have, Karma. And Lily. Not everyone is born with a sophisticated palate. Can you blame those who simply aren't raised any better?

KARMA: Yes!

(I am making a mental note to never, NEVER mention the taco and root beer dinners I have with Charlotte.)

VERONIQUE *(daintily biting into a white truffle and cucumber sandwich)*: You look pensive, Lily. Something on your mind?

ME: Oh. No, no. I was just thinking about my friend Charlotte, that's all.

KARMA: Who's Charlotte?

ME: She's my—she's this girl I know. We've been at school together forever, or whatever. She's away, though.

CHARLES: Anywhere interesting?

ME: Oh, well . . . she's at Young Executive Camp. It's for developing corporate skills, and brainstorming, and learning about business and stuff.

KARMA *(putting her hair up in a twist and securing it with a twig)*: Hah! Good one. Young Executive Camp.

ME: No, she really is. It's true.

KARMA *(looking at me as if I've levitated 2 feet off the ground)*: You can't be serious. A camp for baby capitalists? That's APPALLING!

ME: It is? I mean, is it? I mean, I did kind of wonder—

KARMA: As if the world isn't twisted enough already, they're training teenagers to nickel-and-dime their employees, to reduce benefits and cut corners and lobby to repeal any law that doesn't help them make a buck so they can profiteer by living off the lifeblood of the working poor and destroying the ozone layer in the process?

(When she puts it that way, it really does sound rather bad.)

ME: Yeah, well, I mean, *I'd* never go. She actually wanted me to go with her, but you know. As if.

KARMA: Well you're not like other people, Lily. You're

better than that. But this girl sounds like a real loser.

(I am saved from responding when I drop a mouth-ful of half-chewed Puget Beauty strawberries onto my $81 pants.)

ME: Argh!

VERONIQUE: Oh, let me help!

(She dabs at my stain with a mixture of salt and club soda.)

(Could I be ANY more of an idiot?)

KARMA: Veronique can get any stain out.

(It is getting better as she dabs.)

VERONIQUE: There. Now just make sure to put a stain remover on them when you get home, and soak them in cold water with a little salt right away. They're adorable pants, by the way. I meant to say something earlier. Excellent taste, Lily.

KARMA: We got them together at Fioluzzi. Doesn't she look slamming?

(Slamming!)

VERONIQUE: I thought I recognized that tiny Italian stitching. You know, it really warms my heart to see a young person other than Karma who appreciates quality. I look around at other girls Karma's age wearing raggy old jeans and it breaks my heart. Where is their soul? Where is their sense of excellence? But you, Lily, you have it. You have sophistication and refined taste. Finally! I'm with a teenager who understands the elegance of Italian hand-sewn pants and enjoys squash blossoms stuffed with eggplant caviar. You restore my faith in the next generation, Lily. You really do!

(I felt so, so good at that moment. In spite of the little twinges of guilt I felt having just been thinking that the eggplant caviar was sort of slimy and that the Italian pants were pretty constricting around the thighs and waist and butt—all those tiny stitches, I guess. And for agreeing with them when they dissed Charlotte's camp. But Charlotte called them criminals, so fair's fair, right? And Veronique didn't need to know my pants kind of hurt to wear, and Charles didn't need to know that I was actually scared to be trespassing on private property, and Karma didn't need to know that I did, in fact, plan to write everything that happened down in my notebook later. My secrets were all safe, and I was sophisticated. I had taste. I'm also some nuclear shade of red.)

CHARLES: I hope your parents aren't planning on leaving you alone all summer.

ME: Oh, no. I mean, I'm enjoying the break and everything, especially hanging out with you—

CHARLES: Which we will continue to do on a very regular basis.

ME: Oh, yeah! Great! But no, we do have our usual

summer vacation planned.

KARMA: Excellent. Somewhere important, I hope? Paris? Africa?

ME: Ah. I'm not sure if we'll actually be . . . getting over-seas or anything. We could, I just don't . . . We just have this thing we've done forever, at our lake house. I mean, we kind of have to, I guess. It's our house, and my parents feel like we've got to use it a bit in the summer, you know. To make it worthwhile.

> (*Karma has resumed her methodical consumption of Puget Beauty strawberries and rose-petal ice cream. She's not looking at me. I want to kick myself! Why, why must I always open my mouth and show Karma how stupid I am? I should have just said we were planning on going to Africa, but we hadn't settled on the dates yet. Was there anything uncooler than a lake house?*)

CHARLES: Sometimes it amazes me that we live in a country so wealthy that people have second and third houses that sit empty while there are homeless people in the streets.

ME: Oh, I—

CHARLES: Oh, I don't mean YOUR little lake house, Lily, heavens not. Are there people living there for the rest of the year when you're not using it?

ME: Well, not actually. We did have tenants renting a few

years ago, but it ended up being kind of a hassle for my parents. So now we just close it up.

(And suddenly I think we're exactly part of the prob-lem. Closing our house up! Wasting all that space. I turn that nuclear red again.)

VERONIQUE: Oh, that's nothing, that's not the sort of thing Charles is talking about. A little lake house that's closed up is not draining our resources, using electricity and oil and so forth. Charles means vacation homes that are mansions, staffed year round and filled with gadgets that require gas and electricity to run, and parking lots that pave over the ecosystem, all so some billionaire can spend forty-eight hours there once every six months.

ME: Oh, I know! I read about this guy who is building a vacation home in the Hamptons the size of a shopping mall, with parking for sixty cars! Ours is nothing like that. It's just a cottage, really.

(But Karma is still not saying anything. Is the cottage p.c.? Or is it ultra p.c. because it doesn't squash the ecosystem? I just want to be right! How do I know what is right?)

CHARLES: How many bedrooms?

ME: Just two.

(I glance at Karma. Is that a good thing? Just two? Bad thing?)

CHARLES: Indoor plumbing?

ME: Yes. I mean, there's one bathroom and shower.

CHARLES: Eat-in kitchen? Washer and dryer?

(I'm not sure what he's getting at. Am I giving the right answers or the wrong ones? Since I have no idea, I might as well just be consistent and stick with the truth.)

ME: Well, yes we do have those, but we really don't—

CHARLES: There you have it, then. You, Lily, have a perfectly reasonable vacation home that is adequate but obviously modest and well within the bounds of environmental limitations.

KARMA: See? I told you.

(Relief! A word from Karma, and she's agreeing with her father—I've passed the environmental test, and since protecting the environment is important and I passed the test, the lake house is therefore . . . cool!)

CHARLES: Oh, Veronique, that reminds me—we've got to call the hotel and make those arrangements. It's regrettable, I certainly know. But there's nothing to be done about it.

VERONIQUE: It just goes against our beliefs, Charles.

CHARLES: It's important to our work, Veronique. Ultimately, the end justifies the means, as you know.

(I shoot Karma a questioning look.)

KARMA: Lily is family, Charles. If you're going to talk about this in front of her, it's only polite to let her know what it is you're discussing.

(I can't help it. I get this little happy quiver every time one of the LeBlancs says I'm family.)

CHARLES: Of course you're right, Karma. It's nothing to worry about, Lily. It's just that we've volunteered our home for some environmental tests. We're allowing a group of eco-investigators full access to our house and property, because if there is any chance their tests come up positive, it could have a widespread impact on the chemical- and waste-removal legislation for our state, which I'm sure you know is currently very damaging.

ME: Yes. Yes.

(What? What?)

CHARLES: Unfortunately, the tests themselves are unhealthy to humans, so we need to leave our home for two weeks. I'm pleased and honored to be able to facilitate these tests, especially if the results indicate that companies in our area have been damaging our environment and endangering our lives with the way they discard chemicals and other wastes into the soil. Although the idea of all those extra resources we'll be tapping into at the hotel, the detergent and electricity and oil the hotel uses, is distressing to me. Quite distressing. To think that in endeavoring to stop the problem, I must add to it. Not to mention the expense of the hotel itself, money that could be used directly for Hug the Planet programs, money that could be saving dolphins from tuna nets, or repopulating endangered species.

(I am distressed, too. Poor Charles! All he ever tries to do is the right thing for the world, and things always seem to turn into problems! Why, why are the terrible mansion builders the ones who get rewarded in life, and the truly caring, selfless people like the LeBlancs the ones who spend all their money trying to save the world and get nothing good in return? The LeBlancs are trying to save the world, but who is trying to save the LeBlancs?)

CHARLES: Don't look so down, Lily, it's really fine! It's only for two weeks. We'll make up for the financial loss and the environmental strain somehow. Life is about sacrifice. If you can't or won't sacrifice until it hurts, you'll never make anything of yourself, and you'll certainly never improve the world.

(I start to get the glimmer of a thought, a pre-idea. But whatever it is is interrupted by the sound of shouting. I look around. There's a uniformed man walking briskly toward us, and he's got a huuuuge German shepherd with him.)

UNIFORMED MAN: You there! You people! Can't you read? This is private property, and you are trespassing!

CHARLES *(rolling his eyes)*: Trespassing is a subjective and inaccurate interpretation of the extent to which the law can be applied to the natural resources of our world. I don't acknowledge trespassing as a crime, because I don't acknowledge the right of one human being to bar access to land from another human being.

(I'd like to yell something like "Yay, Charles," but I'm paralyzed by the sight of the German shepherd, and I'm really nervous. Did I mention it is a big, big dog?)

UNIFORMED MAN: I don't care what you acknowledge or not, buddy. My job is to enforce the law on this property. You can get your wife and daughters out of here pronto, or I'm calling the cops and having you hauled down to the station. It's as simple as that.

(Karma gets up, looking extremely bored. Uniformed man thinks Karma and I are sisters! Yay!)

KARMA: What-eeeeever. I'm done anyway.

(She starts walking back toward the street, and I have to say, she looks like a queen. Her head is held high, her back is straight, she's taking long steps, her hair is streaming back off her shoulders. She looks like Angelina Jolie in Tomb Raider. *Like, wow.)*

VERONIQUE *(also getting up)*: I want you to know I don't blame you. You simply don't know any better. One day, if we have the time, perhaps we can enlighten you as to the reality of our responsibility to the environment.

UNIFORMED MAN: The only thing I want enlightened is

this property—by your butts getting off it.

CHARLES *(also walking away)*: In the words of Chief Seattle, "The rocks and meadows all belong to the same family."

UNIFORMED MAN: Yeah, that's right. The VanderHeyden family. The ones who pay my salary. *(Charles continues walking)* Hey, you can't leave all this stuff here! Littering is against the law, too, you know!

(Charles doesn't stop walking. I realize it is my turn to step in and take action.)

ME *(starting to collect our plates and napkins and stuff everything into the LaBouche & Garibaldi shopping bag)*: I'm doing it, I'm doing it. But you have no idea who you were talking to. That's Charles LeBlanc! He's a very, very important environmentalist, and he's dedicated his life and every penny he has to making the world a better place!

UNIFORMED MAN: Yeah, yeah. That doesn't make him above the law.

(I harrumph with irritation. But it is not my job to educate this man or try to save him. Not today, at least. I finish stuffing our garbage into the shopping bag and run to catch up with the LeBlancs, who have reached the street and are still walking. The German shepherd barks in a menacing way. That's one way to end a picnic fast.)

Home again.

5:50 p.m. So much happened today. Already, after just a few hours with the LeBlancs, I feel myself growing. Changing. Becoming . . . less uninteresting. But I need to DO something! Growing isn't enough. What am I doing with my life? Why am I sitting here scribbling every little thing down in this stupid book when there are lunkheads in uniforms with attack dogs policing the earth and violating the moral code of Mother Earth? Sure, maybe I'm going to be a famous writer someday. When I've lived. When I'm worthy. But what about NOW? How do I justify my existence NOW?

I can't stop thinking about what he said, about people having second and third homes when there are homeless people in the world. Why did I never think about that before? I mean, it really is outrageous. And even though Charles tried to make me feel better about our lake house, I think my family is just as much to blame as, say, Donald Trump or somebody like that. I mean, here we have this perfectly good house with insulation and a roof and indoor plumbing, and it sits empty for almost the entire year. And at the same time, there are people who don't have anywhere to live. It isn't right. My own parents are, like, earth beaters. Why can't they be like Karma's parents? They're always doing things, always taking action.

Like founding Hug the Planet, or letting those scientists do those tests at their house. While the only thing I do is sit home and scribble words. What good are words in the face of world destruction?

What would the LeBlancs do if they owned the lake house? Probably charter a bus and collect a bunch of homeless people and drive them up there. Give them the key. Give them a break in life. Could I do that? Would I dare? Oh, let's be real, F.B.s. There's just no way. I don't have that kind of backbone, I don't have the know-how. First of all, where would I charter a bus? How would I fill it with homeless people? I can't. I can't do it. I can't even drive. I'M USELESS! I am aiding and abetting the destruction of our planet by enabling a perfectly good house to remain empty because I don't have it in me to get some needy person living there. I am of no help to anyone. I am not capable of doing anything good.

Or . . . am I?

Thursday, July 11
The miserable Blennerhassett dinner.

It's becoming more and more clear to me, especially after this ridiculous dinner episode. My parents are useless. They will never, never understand what people like the LeBlancs are all about, and they will never understand why I want to be the same way. You can't believe what my parents put me through tonight, F.B.s.

My mother put this plate of meat loaf in front of me. Meat loaf! The operative word being "meat." And I just said it straight out. That I couldn't eat it. And my mother gets this anxious look and starts asking if I'm feeling sick and putting her hand on my forehead and all sorts of ridiculous stuff like that. So obviously I had to *spell* it out for them, and I said it had meat in it! And my father is like Yeah, it's traditional to put meat in meat loaf, and he starts chuckling and slapping the table, and I'm sorry but I just lost my temper. I had to inform my parents that an animal died for that meat loaf, when the earth is capable of providing us with any number of nutritional food items that do not involve the incarceration and execution of innocent living creatures. Then my father starts in with this garbage about meat eating being natural, part of the life cycle and the way we get the nutrients we need. DUH! What does he think VITAMINS are for? But he wouldn't listen to me, neither of them would listen to me! They just went on about how animals kill animals for meat, and humans doing it is just a basic part of existence on earth. Urrrrghhhh!!! Like, a shark can just amble off to the Grand Union and buy a steak! So then my father says, "So it's okay to eat meat as long as you don't buy it?" Can you believe the STUPIDITY? These are not people who will ever understand the destruction of forests, the hunting of practically extinct species, the plight of the homeless, because they can't even get it through their thick skulls that we must all become vegetarians!

So I left the table. I just left. What else could I have done?

10:40 p.m. It's come to me like a dream. Something that I can do. My gift to the planet. We have an empty second house, and the LeBlancs need a place to stay. Future Biographers, you do the math.

I can so, so not WAIT to tell Karma! She'll be so grateful, she'll be so happy, she'll think I'm the best!

Sometime Around Dawn. Most fabulous dream . . . me and Karma took one of the new inflatable motorboats and motored out during stormy seas to rescue a pair of mother/baby humpback whales that had been trapped in a fishing net. Karma held the boat steady, and I leaped into the water holding my knife between my teeth and swam to the net, and the whales understood I was trying to help and stopped struggling. And I cut and cut and cut, and before long the mother and baby were free, swimming joyfully away, and a news helicopter had been hovering overhead and filmed the entire thing, and when Karma and I got back to shore there were thousands of people waiting and cheering, and we were interviewed and celebrated and wined and dined and fabulous boys wanted to date us and fabulous girls wanted to BE us. Going back to sleep right now to try to continue dream.

Friday, July 12

Of all times for Charlotte to call. I was trying to get out of the house to meet the LeBlancs and tell them my idea. I know, I could have just called the HTP office, but to be truthful, I wanted to see their faces when I told them. I was really, really psyched. And I was about to head out the door when Charlotte called.

She was excited about some award she'd won. I felt happy for her, I honestly did, but like I said, I was eager to get going, and I guess I sounded impatient. She asked me what was up, and I explained I was running out to meet the LeBlancs. And then she said something like "Why do you keep hanging out with those people? After what they did? You know your parents don't like them, and no wonder!" Those people? And since when is it unusual to like people and things my parents don't? I don't know, I just felt irritated. I guess I hung up the phone kind of quickly. Like I said, I had to go.

I went right up to the office. They must have been on a conference call or talking about confidential stuff, because the door was locked, and it took a while after I knocked for it to open. Karma looked like she was about to be dismissive until she saw it was me. She said she thought I was another guy passing out menus from the local Chinese takeout, which I thought was pretty funny.

They explained they had all been up all night working on an urgent project. Something that had to get done before Congress met, I think. Karma didn't say much about it, and I knew it would have been inappropriate to ask for details. If I were allowed to know, Karma would have told me. I said I had something to tell them. Charles was in the shower and Veronique was freshening up (I guess those employees working late nights are usually the LeBlancs themselves), and while we were waiting, Karma said she had a present for me!! They were earrings made of crystal and silver, with a tiny amethyst stone on each one. They were beautiful. Karma said she saw them in a boutique and thought how perfect they'd look on me, so she just bought them for me! Just like that! She is so sweet.

Finally Charles and Veronique both came into the room, and Karma explained that I wanted to tell them something. And I just out and told them—that they needed a place to stay and we had a lake house, and I wanted them to stay there, for free.

At first Charles looked stunned. He rubbed his hand over the top of his head and shook his head like he couldn't believe it. But then he said that although it was the most generous gesture anyone had ever made for him, he couldn't accept it. Because of my parents, and the way they felt about the LeBlancs. Because however important the

LeBlancs' need, nothing was worth risking my getting into serious trouble. He said he understood my parents were simply interpreting things from their own very closeted and naïve perspective, but it was the way that they felt nonetheless and had to be respected. He simply would not accept the possibility of causing me more difficulties with them. Of course, he would say that. It's just like him. He's willing to make all the sacrifices, but he doesn't expect anyone else to. The whole time he talked, Karma backed him up. "Listen to him, Lily," she kept saying. "He knows what he's talking about. If he says it's not worth the risk to you, then you know he's right."

He was very persuasive. He said that clearly my parents would never agree to the LeBlancs using the lake house, and to make the suggestion to them would only make my own life miserable. He is so sweet! But I've learned a thing or two from the LeBlancs, and I was already one step ahead.

I told Charles that there was a way it could work. I reminded him of what he'd said to me, on the Fourth of July when the LeBlancs had stopped by. He told me then that it was possible to both respect the sensitivity (and STUPIDITY, if you ask me) of my parents and respect my own needs at the same time. That could work now, too! What I was saying, of course, was that my parents DIDN'T HAVE TO KNOW the LeBlancs were staying in the lake house!

It was really simple! They needed only two weeks, and then their own house would be safe to go back to. They could stay for free in the lake house, and even do their laundry in the lake with biodegradable soap to help keep toxins out of the earth, and no one would ever be the wiser!

Charles still looked doubtful, but at that point, Veronique spoke up. She said I'd obviously done a great deal of thinking about it. She told Charles that he himself had said only last night what an intelligent and resourceful girl Lily Blennerhassett was. And she said that with this incredible gesture, I was proving that I was worthy to be on the LeBlanc team. Then she gave Charles this really intense look, and said, "I think we need her on the team. Come on. What do you say?" Let me tell you, F.B.s, that Charles was really adamant about not accepting my offer. But Karma, Veronique, and I joined forces, persuading and cajoling.

And finally, Charles said okay.

Charles said that their new unexpected housing situation changed many things, and he had to make phone calls, cancel his hotel reservations, advise the environmental test people of his new plans, and stuff like that. Karma offered to walk me to my bus stop. First she made me put on my new earrings. Then she reached into her bag and pulled out one of those clippy combs. With one little movement, she had clipped up my hair into a

French twist. When I looked in the mirror, I couldn't believe it. I looked . . . really good. How did Karma always know how to make me look better?

It was sunny out on the street. It felt good to be walking with Karma. She was looking exceptionally gorgeous. Her hair was down, and she was wearing a black muscle tee, black denim jeans with purple embroidered swirls around the ankles, and biker boots. And she wore a chain around her neck, not a dainty girl chain but a chain chain. It might have been a dog collar or something. It was totally hot.

I was happy, and when Karma linked her arm through mine as we walked, I felt like the day was absolutely perfect. I had done something for someone. I had helped the LeBlancs, who were kind and important people, and in doing so I was helping their own work to save the environment. And Karma had given me a present, and now we were walking down the street arm in arm. I would have broken out in song, but that would have been doofus-y.

We were almost to the bus stop when we passed this little group of kids about my age—two preppy girls and a skinny boy. Just as we went by them, one of them said something like "Ooooo! Look at the girrrrrrrrlfriends!" We continued walking, and I wouldn't even have looked back, but then Karma leaned toward me with this little smile and said, "Want to have some fun?" And well, yes, I said, I did. I didn't know what she had in mind, but I trusted her, so when Karma wheeled around suddenly and started walking back to the kids, I went right with her. She reached up and unhooked the chain around her neck, and she walked straight over to the kids, holding the chain in one hand and slapping it into her other palm.

"One of you have a problem with me and my friend walking down the street enjoying each other's company?" Karma asked.

The three shook their heads violently in unison. One of the girls looked like she might cry.

"Well, I heard one of you make a smart comment about us, and I didn't like it," Karma said, smacking the chain as she spoke. "Which one of you was it?"

They just stared, all three of them, their eyes like saucers. Finally one of the girls said, "It was this other girl, she was just here but she ran into that store."

Karma just stood there, smacking her chain. The girl who had almost been crying started crying for real.

"You tell your friend with the mouth that the next time she or any of you say something unpleasant about me or my friend here, there's going to be a very unfortunate scene. Do you understand?"

The three of them began nodding rapidly.

Then Karma took my arm again, and we walked away. When we got to the bus stop, Karma started to laugh. "They scared so easily! What did they think I was going to do, chain them to each other?"

And then I started laughing, too, and when the bus came and I got on, I was still laughing.

An Afterthought:

Should I stop writing everything down? Who do I think I am, Harriet the Spy? What makes me so great that F.B.s should even be spending their time researching me? F.B.s, I suggest you switch your field of research to the environment, and use this notebook that I am now ONLY keeping to get the credit for an Advanced English summer project to learn more about the LeBlancs' extraordinary work on behalf of our planet.

I guess as long as I put stuff about the LeBlancs in here, it's not a complete waste case. As soon as the summer is over and I hand in my work, no more notebook writing. Write less, DO more!

Saturday, July 13
Rob's Diner.

1:10 p.m. Karma just left the diner. She and I had plans to meet here so I could get her the key to the lake house, and my list of directions and instructions about where things are and stuff. I sort of thought we'd be able to hang out longer than we did. But she had to go. And since I told my mother I was going to the movies, I need to kill some time before going home. Just as well I have my notebook in my backpack, right, F.B.s?

What an ordeal to get out of the house! Pretending to find out where the movie was playing, and going through the motions of making a fake telephone call to check the showtimes, writing the fake movie time down on the memo pad by the phone. Pumping up the tires on my bike and cycling to the bus stop, which is over two miles away. Double locking the bike and counting the change I collected from a) Lenny's change pile on the bookshelf; b) the pockets of everyone's raincoats; and c) the ceramic ashtray that is never used as an ashtray but instead works well as a collector of stray metal objects that sits next to the microwave on top of *The Joy of Cooking* in the kitchen. Rushing for the bus.

And finally, squinching into a nice corner booth. (As a writer, Former Future Biographers and Former Future

Editors, I feel I should be given some flexibility in word making. I know it is not in the dictionary. But I assure you, I did in fact squinch into the booth. This word describes the act of leaning slightly back and extending your legs in front of you as you ease your body into a booth of a diner in which the table is slightly too close to the banquette for comfort. I offer as precedent Kay Thompson's *Eloise*, in which the words "sklonk" and "skibble" are introduced. I am sure that all you Former Future Biographers have sklonked and skibbled at least once.)

Do the diner decorators all work out of one manual?

DINER DECORATION AND DESIGN MANUAL:
1) Red vinyl-covered banquettes.
2) Formica-covered table.
3) Salt and pepper shakers with convenient Sweet 'n Low and sugar-packet holder in the middle.
4) Paintings of Greek scenes hung sporadically around the walls.
5) Counter seats with little round pads in the same red vinyl.
6) Bathroom stalls where the doors do not quite shut all the way.

Because this diner followed those instructions to the letter.

Then Karma arrived. She had on this white tank top

with a black coiled snake on the front of it, and a denim miniskirt, and knee-high boots with a heel. What must it be like to look so good every day? One of the waiters actually dropped his tray when she walked by. When she came and sat down with me, I couldn't resist looking around to see how many people noticed that it was me Karma came to sit with.

The diner didn't have green tea (hello? It's a basic health staple in an educated world!), so Karma ordered us hot water and lemon. She said we could "take our tonics" together. I secretly pretended we were at a spa. Karma says she and Veronique do "mind-body" retreats at spas at least four times a year. Maybe next time I could go with them!

"So, did you bring it?" Karma asked me.

"Oh, of course," I told her, and I took a large envelope out of my backpack. "It's all there," I explained. "I wrote down driving directions for you, and made notes on them about landmarks and stuff. And I wrote a list explaining where everything is, what you do with the garbage, and stuff like that."

Karma spent a minute going through the envelope and nodding.

"Is it okay? Did I leave anything out?" I said. Karma looked up at me.

"It looks fine. Charles and Veronique are really psyched. They said you are totally on the LeBlanc team."

I gave a humble shrug.

"It's like Charles said," I told her. "It's kind of a crime to have a good house standing empty like that."

"Bad karma," she replied. I guess I looked confused, because she went on. "You know, karma. It means all the good or bad vibes you accumulate in life by stuff you do or don't do. You collect your own personal share of good vibes, which will later on bring you good stuff you don't expect. But you also collect your own share of bad vibes, which will bring bad times down on your head out of nowhere."

What a concept. I wanted to believe Karma had come up with it on her own, and named it after herself. But the small part of my brain that had been actively paying attention in last year's World Cultures and Civilizations class had a vague recollection that the concept of karma had predated my Karma. In India or something. Whatever. You didn't catch Lenny and Phyllis throwing the word around. Or Charlotte, for that matter.

"I gotta hop," Karma said suddenly, standing up and tucking the envelope into her bag. "Sorry to sip and split, but HTP calls."

"Oh, can I come up to the office and help out? Stuff envelopes or something?"

"We don't have any mailings going out right now,"

Karma said. "Thanks anyway, though. I'll catch you later. And hey," she added, hoisting her bag and starting out the door, "don't let them charge you for that hot water and lemon. That's bogus. The earth provides those things. They can't be bought or sold."

And then she was gone. And I'm still here, writing like a pod brain from the Planet Suckup.

1:40 p.m. I think they want me to leave. Two of the waiters keep coming by and asking if I want something else, and when I say no, they just stand there. Karma wouldn't be intimidated by that, so I'll try not to be either.

I'm in a bad mood. I guess I feel a little disappointed that after all my machinations and preparations, my actual meeting with Karma lasted only five minutes. I had imagined us lingering over our lemon and hot water for hours, discussing logging issues and whaling situations and generally acting in a spiritually expanding kind of way.

But that selfish thing is kicking in again. I'm just feeling jealous because Hug the Planet is more important for Karma's time than me (and it should be! It absolutely SHOULD be!). And I'm also feeling jealous because I can't help, because I'm an unschooled suck-up-to-the-English-teacher writer with no nonprofit environmental watchdog organizational experience. Which is MY problem, MY character flaw, MY fault. Write less, DO more!

1:50 p.m. My suggestion to the waiter that the hot water and lemon be provided without charge was met with a long and darkly threatening stream of words in a language that may or may not have been Greek. It was certainly Greek to me. Bowing my head in shame, Former F.B.s, I must admit that I forced a laugh and told the waiter that "I was just kidding! Of course I mean to pay."

2:00 p.m. The waiter is asking me to leave.

2:01 p.m. Leaving.

108

Saturday, July 13
An unwelcome postdinner musical interlude.

My father is listening to something truly awful called the Nitty Gritty Dirt Band. He's been trying to pal around with me since the Meat Loaf Incident (apparently still not realizing that it is He and Mom who are the perpetrators of that Meat Crime). He keeps cranking up the volume and saying, "Come on, give it a try!" and shuffling around like he's the genetic offspring of George W. Bush and Janet Jackson. I have pulled down the living-room shades so that he cannot be seen from the sidewalk. This is just so terribly, sadly uncool. If this sort of behavior is discovered, it's I who will pay the consequences. I'll be marked with the Scarlet D and branded a Doofus forever.

Need I even mention that both Charles and Veronique read *Rolling Stone* and are entirely familiar with MTV's top ten videos? I'm sure, F.B.s, that you already suspected. I feel overwrought with hopelessness and despair. Lenny is centuries behind Charles. He is beyond help. He cannot be rehabilitated. He thinks Britney Spears is a kind of specially imported English asparagus.

My browser has frozen at www.duh.com.

Sunday, July 14
Home.

No word from Karma. I tried calling her, but the phone number I have for Hug the Planet is constantly busy. Ma ybe it's out of order. Probably it's just Charles working, working, working. I think there was some kind of big project they were trying to complete at Hug the Planet. You wouldn't expect a person like Karma to stop important environmental work to call and yak with some girl. Plus I'm sure HTP phones are off limits for personal calls.

Monday, July 15
Still home.

No word from the LeBlancs. I miss them. I wish I could go just hang out. See what Karma and Veronique are wearing today. Learn something meaningful about the planet from Charles. But obviously, they are getting their stuff together to move into the lake house. And all those arrangements have to be made to get the environmental testing started. Paperwork has to be signed, probably. They are busy. Why do I only ever think of myself?

I got *Buddhism for Dummies* from the library.

Tuesday, July 16
STILL home.

I will not write in my notebook today because I am not interesting enough to write about, and I can't write about the only interesting people I know, because I haven't seen or spoken to them today. So no writing.

That's final.

THE TOP TEN WORST ITEMS IN MY CLOSET:

10) Cowl-neck sweater knitted with tiny stitches that tend to snag earrings and cause wearer to constantly become frozen with her head bent down toward her shoulder.

9) High-waisted khaki pants that have to be worn rolled up because they were too long when they were bought and for some reason if you don't have things taken up before actually wearing them, you lose the option of having them taken up forever and ever.

8) White shirt with ruffle and Peter Pan collar and built-in restarchifier guaranteeing that no matter how old the shirt is and how many times it has been washed, it will still look and feel about as comfortable as a petrified doily with sleeves.

7) Red blazer with fake-gold buttons and shoulder pads, which is intended to make the wearer look "professional" but instead makes the wearer look like a ticket taker in a movie theater wearing a uniform made for a much older boy.

6) White-and-tan chunky sneakers.

5) Belt made of three strands of imitation leather braided together and ending in a tassel that is

intended to hang down as ornamentation but that frequently results in the wearer having the tassel yanked as the perpetrator shouts, "Ding dong!"

4) Lime-green beret with felt lining. (I know it sounds like it could go either way. Just trust me.)

3) Corduroy pants that immediate maternal ancestor insists fit "perfectly" but in point of fact hit significantly above the ankle, causing them to fall into the nerd fashion category of "high-waters." Also, flap over zipper is permanently bent back, causing zipper to be exposed at all times, provoking needless comments from others.

2) Allegedly dressy sweater crafted in bright red with puffed sleeves and gathered at the bottom, fastened together with large, handmade buttons, each in the shape of a different fruit. The disdain and laughter dispensed upon the wearer of this sweater by peers and society in general are Unprecedented in their Ferocity, Volume, and Length.

1) Slightly wrinkled floor-length shiny green dress with puffed sleeves and a lace collar. Skirt portion has one hidden pocket, inside which has been stuffed a used cocktail napkin bearing the words DELIA AND NED in gold script across the front.

List addendum—articles discovered smushed at the back of underwear drawer:

1) one (1) set of jacks and superball in leather pouch with drawstring.
2) one (1) eyeshade with DELTA AIRLINES printed on the front.
3) one (1) ticket stub to the first Harry Potter movie.
4) two (2) fluff-encrusted LifeSavers, possibly berry flavored.
5) one (1) miniature canoe with CAMP MIGAWAM painted on the side.

Still no calls.

Friday, July 19

I had to take some kind of action before the weekend, when Lenny and Phyllis will both be home.

So I scrounged up some more change and went all the way down to Hug the Planet to say hi to the LeBlancs.

But the office is closed up and locked. No one seems to be there at all. Probably most of the employees are in the field, untangling plastic six-pack rings from the legs of blue herons. Not everybody has nothing to do on a Friday, after all. Some people have entire species to save. Unlike me.

Sometimes, former F.B.s, I feel so ashamed of the meaningless person I am.

Saturday, July 20

Nothi WAIT PHONE IS RINGING!!!!!!!!!!!!!!!

Faithful Transcript:

ME: HELLO?!!!!

CHARLOTTE: Well, at least you sound excited.

ME: Charlotte?

CHARLOTTE: The one and only.

ME: I thought it— Yeah. I mean, hi!

CHARLOTTE: You usually call the day I get home.

ME: Today?

CHARLOTTE: Yesterday. Morning.

ME: Oh, right. No. I mean . . .

CHARLOTTE: You forgot.

ME: I not—didn't . . . there was . . .

CHARLOTTE: You forgot I was coming home.

ME: I . . .

CHARLOTTE : . . . forgot.

ME: Had the wrong day written down.

CHARLOTTE: Whatever.

ME: No, I mean, yay! You're home! I'm sorry, I'm sorry I mixed up the dates. I can't believe you're home! And you have NO idea how glad I am to hear from you! I've been going out of my head with boredom. I was hanging out with Karma—remember I mentioned her?

CHARLOTTE: The one with the criminal parents.

ME: Very funny. It was one late-night swim. Anyway, I've been hanging out with her and her parents a lot—they have this environmental group that's really cool, but then they had to move because of some testing and I haven't been able to get in touch with them and it's making me crazy because I have nothing to do!

CHARLOTTE: And that is the reason you're glad to hear from me? Because your new friend has skipped town?

ME: Nobody's skipped—she's not my—of COURSE not! I totally missed you!

CHARLOTTE: Okay, okay. I missed you, too, like you wouldn't believe. Looking forward to tacos and root beer? How about tonight?

ME: I . . . oh. I can't.

CHARLOTTE *(starting to sound irritated)*: Don't tell me. You have plans with Criminal Girl.

ME: Don't call her that! And no, that's not what I mean. It's the tacos. I don't . . . I'm a vegetarian. Now. I'm a vegetarian now.

CHARLOTTE *(snorting)*: You have got to be joking.

ME: Why do I have to be joking? What's wrong with being a vegetarian?

CHARLOTTE: Why would you suddenly become a vegetarian?

ME: Why wouldn't I? Lots of people are vegetarian. Karma and her parents are.

CHARLOTTE *(in her know-it-all voice)*: Ahhh. Karma and her parents. Uh-huh. I understand now.

ME: What's that supposed to mean?

CHARLOTTE: Just that I understand why the sudden change. You're trying to be like Criminal Girl.

ME: STOP CALLING HER THAT! You've never even met her!

CHARLOTTE: Look, just forget about it, okay? So we're canceling the annual taco and root beer dinner forever because you have spontaneously vegi-formed. Fine. Go call your ultratrendy friend and have a meatless meal or something. My mother is calling me. I have to go.

ME: Good-b— *(line is already dead)*

Monday, July 22

No word from Karma. Boredom unbearable. I ended up walking over to Charlotte's yesterday to extend the olive branch. I even brought over an ice-cold six-pack of Diet Barq's root beer and suggested we replace the tacos with peanut butter and jelly sandwiches, and make that our new traditional meal. She still looked a little put out, but she said she was willing to give it a try.

Since she was being more understanding about the vegetarian thing, I took the opportunity to try to explain the swimming-pool story again so Charlotte could see that the LeBlancs were not the irresponsible people she seemed to think, that they were actually totally the opposite. That it was MY parents, not Karma's, who caused the problem by overreacting.

Nobody knows better than Charlotte how peculiar my parents are about following rules and laws, and I did an imitation of my dad going on about how I had violated a trust and the hotel had the right to make their own rules and nobody was above rules because if everybody decided all at once to do away with rules there'd be anarchy and the whole point was there weren't any lifeguards and the hotel could be held responsible if someone were hurt and didn't I know how much the hotels had to pay in liability insurance every year, which was reflected in the room rates, which kept going up because of all the lawsuits people brought.

Anyway, I noticed Charlotte wasn't laughing. She wasn't even smiling. She looked nonplussed. Or plussed. (Rats, which is it, Former Future Editors? Do even you guys know?) But Charlotte said nothing. So I took the bait and said, "What?"

She just gave me one of her First Lady looks, the one that says I-may-not-look-like-I'm-in-charge-but-you-can-bet-I-am-and-I-don't-much-like-the-look-of-YOU.

"What?" I repeated.

"They were right," Charlotte said. She was flipping through a copy of *The Economist* and not making any eye contact.

"Charles and Veronique?" I asked hopefully.

"Your parents," she said.

I made a gagging noise. And Charlotte got up all of a sudden and paced in front of me, in what I immediately recognized was her Harvard Professor Mode.

"In this country, we are suffering from a plague of litigation," Charlotte said. "Litigation, meaning the instigation of legal actions by one party against another. Lawsuits. Suing." She paused, like she was waiting for me to write it down. "Americans have been given a sense of entitlement and at the same time are being relieved of any sense of personal responsibility. Do you know what this means?"

I became aware that my stomach was about to growl. You can stifle a sneeze, smother a cough, even force yourself to silence a hiccup. But there is no force in the known world capable of stopping a stomach that's bent on growling.

"It means," Charlotte was continuing, "that we have been brainwashed into thinking that any little accident we get ourselves into, no matter how stupid, no matter how clearly our fault, is now a vehicle to riches. Get hurt? Hey, you're entitled to money! Americans are being taught that it is their civic right to sue for any reason. Lady buys herself a cup of coffee at McDonald's, and sues them because it's too hot! Guy gets drunk and falls onto the subway tracks and sues the transit authority for allowing him into the subway when he'd had too much to drink!"

There is a word for the sound of a stomach growling. I'll bet even you Former Future Biographers did not know this. The word is "borborygmus." Isn't it a sublimely wonderful word?

"And the law firms make it easy for us. They say, 'Hey, why not sue? You might win a pile of money! And we'll make it easy for you. If you win, we'll take a percentage of your winnings. But if you lose, you don't have to pay us anything. So why not? What do you have to lose?'"

I think it should be noted somewhere that in a remarkable example of literary precocity, Lily Blennerhassett was already using the word borborygmus when only 13 years old.

"And we're all paying for it," Charlotte continued, pacing frenetically. "Every time you go to an amusement park or a hotel or a health club, you're paying for the fact that these establishments get sued all the time by idiots who feel entitled to money they don't deserve. That's why the commercial with the car driving over the ocean has a little message at the bottom that says 'Professional driver: Do not attempt this at home.' That's why the lids of take-out coffee have a warning on them that the contents may be hot. And that, my good friend, is why hotels have rules about who can swim, and at what time."

"Are you finished?" I asked. "Because I'm starving."

I started for the door, and I'd actually opened it before I realized Charlotte hadn't moved. So I turned around and looked at her.

"What's wrong? Aren't you coming?" I asked her.

"You are really unbelievable," she said.

"What are you talking about?"

"Lily, did you hear anything that I just said? Do my opinions matter to you at all? Does my argument have any weight with you? Or were you just waiting for me to finish so you could raid my fridge and then get back to talking about those stupid people?"

Stupid people? Was Charlotte so far removed from

reality that after all I'd said, she thought the LeBlancs were stupid people?

"I'm beginning think I don't really exist to you anymore," Charlotte said. "I think you should probably just go home now, okay?"

What could I do? What would Karma have done? Karma would have stood up for herself. I never stand up to anyone. Karma would have had an answer to every one of Charlotte's questions. Who was I kidding? Karma would never be hanging around with a former Young Executive Camper to begin with.

So I went home.

Wednesday, July 24

No calls. No Karma, no Charles, no Veronique. And now no Charlotte. And SHE's the one who owes ME an apology. Throwing me out of her house.

It is so, so quiet here. The sound of my own thoughts is overwhelming. How could Charlotte just blow me off like that? For what? For being angry at something I did that she didn't even see, and for not liking people she's never even met?

Once, when I was about four or five, I was in a dance class with a bunch of other girls. And one of the girls had this purple splotch across the side of her face. And I remember walking up to her and asking, "Why do you have grape juice on your face?" I don't remember what she said. Maybe she didn't say anything. And I forgot about it until just now, like nine years later. And as I thought about it, just two minutes ago, I suddenly realized that it wasn't grape juice that girl had on her face. It was a birthmark. I must have made her feel bad, even though I had no idea at the time. I don't know what made me remember this.

It's weird how you can look at something and see it a certain way, then out of the blue, for no reason, you all of a sudden know it was something different all the time. That you were wrong, what you thought you saw was wrong, what you said was wrong. Like thinking Charlotte would understand Karma, or be anything better than dismissive of her.

It did look like grape juice, though.

Thursday, July 25
Home again, home again.

I'm getting really, really antsy. And you know, I'm feeling worried about the LeBlancs. I don't know how they're getting on. I haven't heard from them, and all I can think about is satisfying my own curiosity and making sure everything is okay with them. They could have had a wreck on the way to the lake house, or a sinkhole could have developed and swallowed them as they sat on the front porch, or they might have accidentally picked up that flesh-eating disease—

Okay, if you must know the truth, it's that I'm bored. Without the LeBlancs, my life experience is about as rich as a cardboard box under a couch. I am mind-numblingly, bone-crunchingly, life-stiflingly BORED. My parents are stupid. My former friend Charlotte is stupid. My notebook is stupid. Everything here is stupid, and the only known antidote is the LeBlancs. I need to talk to them. I need to see them. I need to exist in their atmosphere and recharge. I want to eat juiced tuberous begonia spritzers and gazpacho with grape foam. I want to shop for Italian leather shoes with sterling silver buckles. I want to LIVE! I have to see them. But how am I going to get in touch, since the phone at our lake house isn't hooked up. (I should have thought of that! How inconsiderate of me to send them to a house with no working phone!)

What am I going to do? I'm losing my mind. I'm losing my spirit. I think I'm beginning to hate me.

Friday, July 26

I have a plan. You may think it unethical, F.F.B.s, to learn that I had to call Charlotte and apologize to her even though I wasn't sorry because I still think she is the one who started the problems between us, but I pretended I was sorry and I made it sound good. That's what Charles would have told me to do, I'm sure. And it paid off, because during our phone conversation, I found out that Charlotte's parents are going to be away until very late Saturday night. So I have casually informed Lenny and Phyllis that I'd like to spend that day with Charlotte and sleep over. Simple!

This will give me the time I need to bike to the train station and take the train up to the lake house. I can drop in on the LeBlancs, sleep over, and come back home Sunday with no one the wiser! Isn't it great? I'm writing my own life like it's a novel!

The only problem is Charlotte. Do I tell her I'm pretending to be at her house, so she can cover for me in an emergency? But then she'll want to know where I'm going. And I can hardly expect her to support my going to visit "those criminal people." She'd certainly try to argue me out of it. And let me tell you, F.F.B.s, arguing with Charlotte is like trying to claw your way out of a pit of Jell-O. It requires an enormous amount of effort and concentration and is still hopelessly impossible, not to mention messy. No, Former Future Editors, I'm sticking with the metaphor. If you don't get it, then you don't get Charlotte. Pit of Jell-O. Wobbling chunks sticking to my shirt and hair.

And. If I tell Charlotte about going to see the LeBlancs, I will be divulging unnecessary details and the whole lake house thing is bound to come out (Charlotte's like an investigative ferret in these conversations), and I REALLY don't want to hear Charlotte's opinion of my letting the LeBlancs temporarily stay at our totally empty and unused vacation home without asking my parents. All sorts of moral and ethical issues will be raised—Charlotte LOVES to throw morals and ethics around. If it were a school sport, she'd be captain of the varsity squad.

I keep thinking about what Karma said about anyone who would actually willingly go to Young Executive Camp. She said something about Charlotte perpetuating the system of profiteering at the expense of the rest of the world. That Charlotte is a baby capitalist, and that if her kind are allowed to take advantage of the rest of us unchecked, it could send the planet into a tailspin. Maybe I can't blame Charlotte for being what she is any more than I can blame myself for being a writer. A former writer. Charlotte obviously doesn't realize that the path she's chosen for herself is selfish and disgraceful and contemptuous of the rest of us. It isn't really her fault she doesn't know that SHE is the problem the LeBlancs are fighting against. And up until this summer, before the LeBlancs helped me see things their way, I thought Charlotte would be my best friend forever. But Karma once said she didn't think Charlotte was the right kind of friend for me. Now I see how right she was. So though I'm sure Charlotte would feel entitled to know what I'm up to, especially since I've tossed her name into the mix, I just can't tell her. A tiny part of me wants to. But I cannot visit the pit of Jell-O today.

Evening Footnote:

My mother is having a small fit. Apparently, she just got a thank-you note from Delia for the wedding gift. The note very politely thanked Lenny and Phyllis for the lovely bird feeder. Problem is, Lenny and Phyllis didn't send Delia a bird feeder. They sent her a very expensive, one-of-a-kind, hand-blown glass pitcher that they bought in Mexico. They've kept it around all year, waiting for the perfect occasion to bestow it upon a lucky person as a gift. Enter Delia and her wedding. Since the pitcher didn't come in a box, Phyllis wrapped it in bubble wrap and put it inside an old box from a bird feeder. I can imagine what happened. Delia ripped the wrapping paper off, saw what appeared to be a bird feeder, and tossed the box onto the "yard sale" pile without looking inside it. The exquisite hand-blown one-of-a-kind pitcher is now destined to languish anonymously until some puzzled, yard-sale-attending bird lover opens the box and wonders what on earth he just paid fifty cents for.

Saturday, July 27
The Blennerhasset breakfast table.

The stage is set. I have informed my parents of my plan to spend Saturday with Charlotte. Phyllis is disappointed, as Saturday is the last day that the Local Amateur Watercolorists Celebrate Regional Pastoral Scenes exhibit will be on view at the library. But both Lenny and Phyllis have been laying off pushing their conventional meaningless stuff on me, since the Meat Loaf Incident. I said I wasn't interested in paintings, and that was that. So I'm good to go.

They look so boring. So standard. Lenny is trying to get a little splitch of milk off his shirt (Former Future Editors: With regard to "splitch," please see prior entry in defense of the word "squinch"). Phyllis has lifted the toaster and is attacking the counter underneath with a sponge and a spray bottle of antibacterial cleanser. Because as we all know, outbreaks of contagious and deadly diseases frequently originate from bread crumbs that are allowed to remain on a kitchen counter for more than twenty minutes after that toast is eaten.

Sometimes I think about time. How strange it is to be aware of something you have no control over. Like, there they are, my parents, Lenny and Phyllis. I'm looking at them while I'm drawing this line in my diary but one day in maybe fifty years or so, they'll be gone. But the line I drew will still be there. Will I still think of them as boring then? Or will it be the line that looks boring in fifty years? My thoughts that look boring? Me that looks boring?

11:23 a.m. I have done it!!!!!!! I am on the train, heading north. In one hour I will arrive, find a taxi, and head over to the lake house. My eventless early-summer existence combined with my natural frugality has paid off, because I had enough allowance put away for a round-trip train ticket, cab fare, and some left over for a bucket of curly fries!

I believe I have thought of everything. I even left my bike behind at Charlotte's house, rather than at the train station where someone might steal it. At last, maybe I'm beginning to think more like a LeBlanc and less like a Blennerhassett!

Soon I'll be there. Won't the LeBlancs be amazed!!!

The Reunion

First I just stood looking at the house for a minute. It always feels great to see it—I get this feeling of happiness and security, because no matter what has happened during the year, or how much the world might seem to be changing, the lake house always looks exactly the same.

It's nothing fancy, our lake house. Just a one-story

cottage, wood clapboards painted white, gray roof, green porch with a hammock. There is a lawn big enough for a game of croquet, and an old birdbath that's been there since, as Phyllis says, the beginning of time. And pine trees everywhere, sloping all the way down to the lake. The good old, cool, simple, always reliably refreshing lake.

It's important to have things to depend on. Things that will always, always be the way you expect, no matter what. I only know two things like that. *Star Trek*, and the lake house.

A Little Dialogue:

ME *(knocking and knocking and calling)*: Hello? Anybody home?
    (Door is locked. I keep knocking.)
ME: Karma? Charles? It's me, Lily! It's Lily!
    (Fumble fumble fumble. Door opens. It's Charles, looking a little rumpled, probably from worry due to environmental testing.)
CHARLES: They called you?
ME: What?
CHARLES: The Whittakers called?
ME: The Whittakers? From across the street? No, they didn't call. I just came up to surprise you! I wanted to make sure everything was okay. That you didn't need anything.

(Pause. Charles looks worried. He could use some more sleep, poor guy.)

CHARLES: You brought your parents?

ME *(a little confused)*: No, I thought we sort of agreed it would be better if they didn't know about this. I took the train.

CHARLES: The train?

ME: To surprise you!

CHARLES: The train! To surprise us! What an excellent surprise! *(Shouting into the house.)* VERONIQUE! KARMA! Lily's here, drop-in surprise!! Stop whatever you're doing and come on down! *(Talking to me again.)* Sorry, Lil, I got a little confused there for a sec. The Whittakers saw the lights in the house and came by a few times asking what we were doing. When you knocked, I thought maybe they called your parents and blew the whistle.

(Charles laughs, and I do, too.)

ME: No, they didn't call. I'll be happy to explain to them it's all on the up and up, your being here.

CHARLES: That'd be great, Lily. I'll wait right here.

(Pause.)

ME: Oh. You mean you want me to go over to the Whittakers' right now?

CHARLES: That'd be great. Karma and Veronique will be waiting when you get back.

(Pause. Well, Charles has always made sense before.

So off I go, and I explain to a very doubtful-looking Mrs. Whittaker that the LeBlancs are family and that our lake house is their lake house. By the time I get back, Karma and Veronique are standing outside. Veronique gives me a huge hug and calls me her honey. But this environmental-testing thing really seems to be taking a toll on everyone. Veronique is wearing a simple Indian print dress, which looks nice but rumpled. And Karma looks washed out! She has on plain running shorts and a faded T-shirt, and her hair is pulled back in a lumpy ponytail with a rubber band. What surprises me most is the expression on her face. If it were anyone else I would have called it sullen, but on Karma I guess I'd call it exhaustion, or stress or something. For a minute, I begin to wonder if I've made a mistake in coming. Then all of a sudden, Charles starts clearing his throat and coughing, and right then Karma gives herself a little shake and grabs me in a big hug.)

KARMA: Can't believe you're here! And not a minute too soon. I've been inside scrubbing out the bathroom, which is why I'm dressed like a washerwoman. Veronique has always had a real problem with people who have to hire someone to clean their house, so I learned how to get a bathroom clean at a really young age.

VERONIQUE: I'm simply not comfortable having that sort

of servant-employer relationship with someone. Watching another human being crouch over your toilet for pay is truly distasteful.

KARMA: Unless that human being is me.

VERONIQUE: Unless that human being is a member of the household who frequently uses the same toilet.

KARMA: But not any member of the household. Not, for example, YOU. Or Charles.

ME: Oh, my mother is the same way! Everything has to be immaculate, but we have to do it! I think mostly it's because my mother couldn't stand the thought of a cleaning lady coming into our house and actually finding things that needed to be cleaned! I mean, what would she think of us!!

(Karma laughs suddenly. Charles and Veronique are having some sort of inaudible exchange, and Veronique follows him into the house.)

KARMA: And how *are* Lenny and Phyllis?

ME: Oh, the same as ever. We had this big war over meat loaf, if you can believe it.

KARMA: Meat loaf? What were they doing with a meat loaf?

ME: Exactly. I wouldn't touch it, and I lit into them about eating meat, and they totally couldn't get it. I was like, whatever. I'm not eating it.

KARMA: That's only the first step, Lily. If you're living in a house where meat loaf is eaten, even if you are not the one eating it, you're still complicit. You're an accessory to that cow's murder. It's easy to change yourself. The hard part is changing other people.

ME: I never thought of it that way.

KARMA: They're just my beliefs.

ME: No, you're totally right! I need to change my parents. *(I laugh.)* What I'd actually like to do is really change my parents. Literally. Like, exchange them for your parents.

KARMA: You've got to work with what you have. It's all about the right beliefs. Right beliefs make right living.

ME: Right beliefs make right living. I wish I could come up with stuff like that. I am so glad I'm here. I was bored out of my mind at home, and then my friend Charlotte got back from camp and we got into this fight and aren't really talking.

KARMA: Your junior-capitalist friend? *(I nod.)* I can't imagine why someone like you would hang out with someone like that, Lily. You're an old soul, and she's a predator-in-training. My parents would freak if I ever brought home someone like that.

ME: No, I totally understand that now. That's why we fought, really. I just can't support who she is. And when I told her about meeting you, and how great you were, she just thought you sounded stupid.

> *(I can't believe I said that. I truly did not mean to let*
> *that last part slip out. Karma looks at me sharply.)*

KARMA: She said I sounded stupid? She's never even met me.

ME: I know! I totally agree, and that's why we're not

speaking, because of that attitude.

KARMA: So she's not your friend now because of me?

ME: Well . . . yeah, I guess that's true.

(Karma smiles at me.)

KARMA: Do not even THINK about telling me you aren't sleeping over tonight.

ME: Definitely!

(What I'd like to add: I'd love to sleep over forever—do you think Charles and Veronique will adopt me? Do you think it's possible Charles and Veronique are actually my real parents, and the story of your long-lost twin sister who was tragically misplaced in an unmarked bassinet at birth meant for the Blennerhassett baby girl can finally be told, and my true identity revealed? May the world learn along with me that Lily is actually a LeBlanc in Blennerhassett clothing?)

KARMA: I'll take that as a definitely yes, I'm sleeping over, not a definitely I'm not.

ME *(laughing)*: Definitely yes. Definitely yes.

Front porch.

5:00 p.m. It is SO different being here without my parents. Veronique doesn't have the obsession with cleanliness that my mother has, and what a relief! (Even though Karma was supposed to be scrubbing the bathroom, I must have interrupted her before she started, because it is definitely not scrubbed at all.) To be somewhere that it's okay to let the dishes lie in the sink, or even right on the kitchen table. To have food that can actually sit out awhile before being attacked with Saran Wrap, labeled, and hidden away in the fridge. Because what is the big deal, after all? Why is it so important to get everything into the dishwasher, wiped down, sterilized, pasteurized, and scoured in every way before a person can even digest a meal? What the LeBlancs understand that the Blennerhassetts don't is that you have to make time to enjoy life! You can't spend every free minute putting everything frantically back in order. Take some time to digest! This is something my mother will never understand.

7:40 p.m. Oh, F.B.s, you'll never guess what we're having for dinner! Karma says it is Appetizer Night! Every once in a while the LeBlancs buy up whatever frozen appetizers take their fancy, and they pop them all in the microwave, and their entire meal is just appetizers! Genius! Genius!!

A SAMPLING OF TONIGHT'S FARE:
Miniature cheddar quiches
Tofu pigs in a blanket
Cheese blintzes
Deep-fried mushrooms

Mozzarella sticks
Veggie pizza pockets

9:00 p.m. The LeBlancs do things European style, and that means eating dinner really late. I don't mind. I'm just getting settled. Charles and Karma were whispering for a while, then Karma came over and really sweetly asked me if I'd mind sleeping on the porch hammock. She said they were doing a lot of HTP work in both of the bedrooms, and there were lots of piles of documents, and also some sensitive materials it was probably best I didn't see. I said I'd be fine on the porch. Karma even found some of our biodegradable soap, and she put it out on the porch for me with a towel, so that I wouldn't have to use the bathroom inside. Finally. I may still be unimportant, but at least I am now surrounded by importance. And I am NO LONGER BORED!

11:40 p.m. That was one of the best dinners I have EVER had! We ate out on the porch, and all the appetizers were just piled together higglety-pigglety and everybody just grabbed what they wanted! No standing on ceremony!

A Little Conversation:

CHARLES: I can't tell you enough times how delighted we are to see you, Lily.

VERONIQUE: Yes, Karma was saying just today how dreadfully she missed you, weren't you, Karma?

ME: Really?

(Karma looks up and around, then nods.)

ME: Yeah, I really missed all of you, too. And I just got to worrying, you know, wanting to make sure there wasn't anything you needed. And dumb me, I sent you to a house where the phone wasn't hooked up . . . so I thought I just better come on up and check myself.

CHARLES: You're a very intelligent and resourceful young lady. But *(and he wagged his finger at me)* I want you to promise not to take another risk like this one.

ME: What do you mean?

CHARLES: We're thrilled to have you here, Lily, but it isn't worth the trouble you might get into if your parents found out. I'm going to make sure to get you to the earliest train in the morning. There can't be any chance of anyone finding out you aren't where you're supposed to be. I'd have sent you back tonight, but Karma explained that you have an alibi. That your parents think you're sleeping over at a friend's.

ME: Which I am! It isn't even a lie. It is totally fine, I promise. There is no way for my parents to know I'm here. And I have a schedule, there's a train at 7:50 in the morning. I'll just need to go to the Whittakers' to phone the taxi company.

CHARLES: No, no. Wouldn't hear of it. I'll drive you myself.

ME: You don't have to do that.

KARMA: Don't sweat it, Lily. He wants to take you.

ME: Thanks, then.

CHARLES: But we'll be much better this time about keeping in touch. When is a good time for one of us to call you, when we're not likely to disturb your parents?

ME: Well, weekday late mornings are usually a good time.

CHARLES: Then you just sit tight, Lily, my dear. We won't let you stay all alone in that house for too long. There are a lot of wonderful things we can do.

ME: I was sort of hoping you might teach me the business.

KARMA: The business?

ME: I know I don't have a degree or anything. I don't even have any skills. But I just want so much to be able to help out with your work. To help the environment.

CHARLES: Ah, the environment! A very kind offer, Lily.

VERONIQUE: Tofu pig in a blanket? Mozzarella stick?

(Karma says something about being sick of cheese, or feeling sick from the cheese. She goes outside.)

VERONIQUE: Poor thing, she's been feeling rather miserable, Lily.

CHARLES: Getting over a stomach flu.

VERONIQUE: And overworking herself and never seeing anyone her own age. What a bit of serendipity you came to visit!

144

CHARLES: Serendipity indeed. You're the only friend of Karma's I've ever felt was worthy of her, Lily. And that's saying something.

(I continue to eat assorted appetizers and bask in the glow of the LeBlancs' all-encompassing love and praise. Happy, so happy, at last. I would be happier if Karma herself were still at the table, witnessing and contributing to the love and praise. But she obviously seems moody only because she is tired and lonely and had to scrub the bathroom, which makes her condition implicitly my fault since if I were a person of worth, I would have scrubbed that bathroom myself.)

Midnight Note:

I'm writing by moonlight. Karma is fast asleep inside, so she won't know I'm being self-indulgent by writing, even if I'm doing so only to get credit for my summer project so I can make Honor Roll, eventually graduate, and go do something meaningful for the planet.

I hate that I have to leave tomorrow. I belong here, with the LeBlancs. I wish they would ask me to stay. But Charles would never do that, because he knows that would cause a problem between me and my parents. Sometimes I wish Charles were just a tiny bit less considerate. But I know he's right. I just wish I could do a life rewind and start over again, this time being born a LeBlanc. Then I might have had a chance.

There's nothing for me to do now but go home and make Lenny and Phyllis see that they have to be vegetarians. I'll do it for all the animals of the world.

And I'll do it for Karma.

Sunday, July 28
On the train.

A successful and thrilling expedition. I adore the LeBlancs more than ever! Do you know what we had for breakfast, F.B.s? Microwave popcorn and hot chocolate. And Karma didn't want to wait for Veronique to get out of the shower, so she washed her hair in the lake, and then I did, too! And two fishermen rowed right near us and Karma waved to them in this flirtatious way, and when they rowed toward us she ran away, shouting "Suckers!" and I ran away and they yelled at us and we laughed and laughed. I had the best time!

I feel that at last I have tasted living, without the rules and boundaries of hygiene, etiquette, and nutrition that my parents have trapped me with for thirteen years! I have been set free! Liberated! I'm a completely new person! Now I know that life can hold something different for me than what my parents have laid out! Because of the LeBlancs, maybe I actually can write a meaningful work one day. Future (no longer Former) Biographers, celebrate July 28 as the spiritual and creative birthday of Lily Blennerhassett, the day on which the future National Book Award and Pulitzer Prize winner took her first real breath in the world!

1:00 p.m. oh i am in so much trouble

Monday, July 29

I just couldn't bring myself to write about it yesterday. As F.B.s undoubtedly knew the whole time, my return did not go as smoothly as I'd hoped. It went about as well as the maiden voyage of the *Titanic*.

I was really worried when I got to Charlotte's house to pick up my bike and saw a police car in the driveway. The crazy thing is, my first thought was "Someone broke into the house last night and kidnaped Charlotte and if I had really had a sleepover there it could have been me!"

So naturally I went straight inside to comfort Charlotte's frightened and grieving parents. Only the frightened and grieving parents I ran into were mine. First they both ran and grabbed me and hugged me. Then, at the same time, both of them started thwacking me over the head, with Phyllis saying something with each *thwack* like "Where *thwack* have *thwack* you *thwack* been *thwack* don't *thwack* ever *thwack* do *thwack* this *thwack* again? *thwack*? (I'm lost on the punctuation here, Future Editors. Does it come before the sound effect or after?)

And I explained. And it was bad. Everyone was so angry. Lenny and Phyllis were angry while trying not to cry. Charlotte was angry while trying not to throttle me. The police were angry while trying not to handcuff me.

148

Charlotte's parents looked angry while also looking relieved that it was someone else's daughter who had behaved in this abominable way.

Another silent ride home in the Honda.

Note to any and all Future Biographers still living at home with their parents: I am now in a position to state that the Single Worst Possible Thing You Can Ever Do is to go off somewhere and not tell your parents where you are. Though it may seem obvious to you and I (you and me?) that if I am not at Charlotte's house, clearly I am SOMEWHERE ELSE, it does not work this way in parent-brain. In parent-brain, if I am not at Charlotte's house, I am dead, dying, disfigured, or all of the above. I beg you to benefit from the miserable experience of Lily Blennerhassett and not repeat this terrible mistake.

Also, if you are planning a secret expedition, do not forget to pack your retainer, leaving it, instead, in plain view in the bathroom, where your mother, in the interests of keeping your teeth straight, will scoop it up and bring it over to Charlotte's house and realize you are not there.

Insomnia.

11:50 p.m. No one will speak to me. I am thoroughly mis-understood, mis-accused, mis-treated, and miserable.

Clarification for Future Biographers:

1:47 a.m. I did, of course, tell them right away where I'd gone. And I didn't technically lie. Not technically. I simply said I'd been with the LeBlancs. It was only when my father tried to find their phone number that I realized they didn't know where I'd been. Of course they didn't know—how could they? They thought I'd gone to the LeBlancs' house. But of course they weren't home, because of the environmental testing. Why there was no listing for them, I cannot say. But it just seemed like the wrong time to mention the little detail about the lake house. I feel certain Charles would have advised me not to bring it up.

Oh, Future Biographers, is it a lie to keep the whole truth to yourself?

Tuesday, July 30

I am a political prisoner, imprisoned and shunned by the civilized world for refusing to abandon my beliefs and my people. I am a proud member of the LeBlanc team, and I am willing to be punished, suffer, and die for it. To be punished and suffer, anyway.

Thursday, August 1

There's no point in even trying to write every day. My parents have gone through the basically meaningless motions of grounding me (again), meaningless because I have nowhere to go (still). Charlotte doesn't want to see me, and at the train station Charles made it very, very clear that he doesn't want me to risk seeing them again, and that was even before I got busted. Which, thankfully, they don't know about. At least they won't have to bear the burden of guilt for the mistakes of my ridiculous family and former friend.

Whatever. It doesn't even matter. What is really awful is the way my parents are treating me. It's this sort of wounded, we-just-don't-understand disappointment. That moment I showed up at Charlotte's house they were head-spinningly furious. Now they're just acting sort of weary.

Is it my fault I've entered a period of moral and environmental enlightenment that my parents are unable to keep up with or even understand? Is it my fault that I have grown spiritually by leaps and bounds, and that my actions far exceed my parents' ability to comprehend? Is it my fault that they refuse to give me the benefit of the doubt, that they insist on thinking "in the box," and that any tiny little thing that departs from their own beliefs is this enormous crime?

You know what? Let them give me their weary, disappointed little looks. Let them keep me grounded until the next Ice Age. Let them disapprove of every single thing I've become. I've decided that Lenny and Phyllis Blennerhassett are hopeless cases. They think that just because they are my parents (if they even ARE—the switched-at-birth thing is a DEFINITE possibility), I am required to think what they think, to wear what they wear, and to have as boring and meaningless a life as they do.

How ridiculous are parents, thinking they can MAKE their children believe and live the way they want them to? Before too long I'll be grown up myself, and out in the world, and living the way I want to. So where is all their tyranny going to get them? No phone calls on Mother's Day, that's what. One good thing, ONE good thing has happened to me this year, and my parents can't stand it. Well, okay! I've got time. I can wait. One day I'll be free, and they'll be SORRY!

You'd think at least Charlotte would be able to understand. Okay, fine, so she thinks she doesn't like the LeBlancs (she can't actually not like them, because it isn't possible to dislike someone you don't know). My bad, then, for failing in my attempt to describe them as they really are. So my parents are lost causes, they're too old. But Charlotte is my age. I should be able to change her. She isn't ruined yet. I have to make her see. I have to make her understand. I have no one left to talk to.

4:00 p.m. Well, I'm allowed to use the phone, so I will. I'm going to call Charlotte. I am. I don't care what she learned at Young Executive Camp—I've known her for eleven years. If she doesn't understand, it's because I didn't try hard enough to make her understand. And the first thing she needs to admit is that she does NOT GET TO BE MAD ABOUT THIS. I'm the one who gets to be mad! I'm the one in trouble, I'm the one suffering for the good I tried to do in the world. Charlotte is not the victim here! Okay. Okay. I'm dialing. I'm dialing right now.

A Little Phone Conversation:

CHARLOTTE *(in her well-tailored-suit–Wall Street Journal tone)*: I don't even know why we're speaking. You obviously don't understand the ramifications of your actions.
   (Translation: You don't get what you did.)
ME: What are you talking about? I apologized to everyone, didn't I?
   (No translation necessary.)
CHARLOTTE: Lily, you've done something bad and now you have to do some listening. You made me your unwitting accomplice.
   (Translation: I, Charlotte, am an innocent young lamb.)
ME: I told them all you didn't know a thing about it!

Didn't I? You're not the one that got punished, right?

CHARLOTTE: First of all, that is irrelevant. The fact is, you made me an accessory. You know that, don't you?

(Translation: Doesn't matter. You did bad things for which there are four-syllable words.)

ME: Of course I know what an accessory is. God, Charlotte. Who taught you the black purse with black shoes, brown purse with brown shoes rule?

CHARLOTTE: That's not the kind of accessory I'm talking about. And in reality, my being your accessory isn't even the central issue.

(Translation: I'm going to make a murky allusion to a word that sounds like an official legal term, then hint at a coming subject change.)

ME: Meaning?

CHARLOTTE: Do I have to spell it out for you?

(Translation: I'm going to have to spell it out for you.)

ME: It's beginning to look that way.

(Sound effects: Pause followed by an audible sigh from Charlotte.)

CHARLOTTE: You've apologized for making plans without telling me. You've apologized for using my name as a cover story. I don't care about those things, Lily. What I care about is that from the moment your mother showed up at my house Saturday night, and we all realized you were missing, I was terrified! When your parents are actually crying, and the police show up in the flesh with guns and everything in your living room, it's pretty flipping scary! I figured, if the grown-ups are all so upset, something bad must really have happened to you! And I believed it, Lily. I thought something bad had happened to you—I was sure. And do you know WHY I was so sure?

(This has the hallmark of a question Charlotte is going to answer herself, so I remain silent.)

Because I knew we were such good friends that it was UNIMAGINABLE that you would be planning something like sneaking off for the night without telling me. I never questioned it! The police even asked me, did I think maybe you'd had a plan to secretly go off somewhere to meet someone. And I told them you hadn't! I told them we were best friends, and there was NO WAY you would have been planning something like that without telling me!

But you didn't, did you, Lily? You have this whole secret life now, something to do with those stupid people, and I'm not important enough to know about any of it. So as a result, I spent the worst night, THE WORST NIGHT OF MY LIFE, Lily!!! Worrying myself sick over what had happened to you. You left your BICYCLE AT MY HOUSE, for heaven's sake!!! What were any of us supposed to think???

And now I know, don't I? Now I know what happened.

And you have the nerve to keep calling me and wondering why I'M the one who's upset. You obviously don't have a clue. And since you never listen to me anymore ANYWAY, I'm not going to talk about it anymore. And I don't want to talk to YOU anymore.

(Translation: Lily bad.)

Friday, August 2

Charlotte doesn't like me anymore.

Saturday, August 3

I guess it's just you and me now, Future Biographers. Remember *A Little Princess*? Sara (who everyone agrees is a very good-hearted girl) loses everything—her parents, her friends, all her stuff. She gets sent up to the attic, which is deserted except for this rat, Melchisedec. And her only friend from the outside world is the little monkey who climbs in from the window next door. I feel like Sara (who is, as we have all agreed, a good-hearted person). My notebook is Melchisedec. And you, my dearest Future Biographers, are the little monkey.

Sunday, August 4

Will I ever see Karma again? What if, by the time I'm finally free of my parents, the LeBlancs have moved off to some organic commune in Tanzania where they commit their days to planting food and administering simple health care to needy people? How will I ever find them? Have I had all of the LeBlancs I am ever destined to have? Will they come look for me? Is it possible I will continue to grow without them, or am I stuck where I am? Can I think my way through this alone? Can I write my way out?

Monday, August 5

Still writing. Still thinking. About the grape juice. And Charlotte. How do you know if a person is the right friend for you? Does it have to be Karma *or* Charlotte? It's not allowed to be both? Charlotte and I learned to crawl together. We did potty training as a team. Karma is cool, and Charlotte is not. Karma is beautiful and different, and Charlotte is . . . Charlotte. Can I not have them both? Do I have to erase Charlotte's friendship because of the new me? Is it because it never had any real meaning, but I only started seeing the truth through Karma's eyes? Maybe that relationship with Charlotte just existed, like the universe. Well, I guess maybe it doesn't exist anymore.

The only thought I keep having is one I don't really like. I'm mad at my parents and Charlotte because they won't listen to me, they won't try to understand what I did and why I did it and who I want to be now. But I guess, if you want to get technical about it, I haven't listened to them and really tried to understand their points of view. Which is only because I know I'm right and they're wrong! But that probably doesn't change the fact that unless I'm going to be a hypocrite, I have to make an honest effort to hear them out and try to understand their feelings.

And THEN I can tell them why they're wrong.

Tuesday, August 6
The Blennerhasset dominion.

I talked to my parents during breakfast. I said I'd been doing a lot of thinking about how worried they must have been. About how long those hours must have seemed between when they realized I was missing and when I showed up. I told them how important the LeBlancs were to me, and how if I was ever going to improve as a person, it was crucial I become more independent and make some of my own choices. Unfortunately, I could not really make my point—which is that I had truly HELPED the world by allowing the LeBlancs to stay at the lake house—because I wasn't actually planning on telling my parents that part. I may be bored and uninteresting, but I'm not stupid.

So I had to make it about the LeBlancs' treating me like an adult, and Karma being such a great role model (parents are supposed to FLIP with happiness when you point out positive role models all by yourself). And then I ended by saying that NONETHELESS I now realized that they had been truly frightened (like Charlotte said) and that I was sorry about that, and that I would never put them through that again.

My mother was a bit teary, though to give her credit she did hold them in (when other mothers might have deliberately squeezed them out for effect). My father was more frozen faced. He was shoveling in mouthfuls of Bran Bonanza like he was getting paid to eat by the bite. My mother said that I'd no idea, NO IDEA, how frightened they'd been (even though I had just said I did know). Then suddenly she started rubbing at her face with both hands, and she shook her head like she didn't want to think about that night, even though it turned out all right. For a minute she still looked about as hysterical as she had when I first walked into Charlotte's house and found the police there. And suddenly I could really see it. For the first time, looking at the two of them sitting there, I felt right down in my stomach how incredibly frightened they must have been when their only child seemed to have vanished without a trace.

Karma and her family are everything to me. But I see now I should have found another way to be with them. Even if it meant telling my parents the truth and defying their instructions to stay away from the LeBlancs. Maybe I should have just faced the music.

Wednesday, August 7

A little better. Still haven't seen Charlotte in person, but the talk yesterday with my parents seems to have helped around here. I'm going to try harder to get myself into other people's shoes and walk around in them. That means I'm going to try to imagine what other people feel like on the inside, F.B.s. Isn't that what writers are supposed to do? Imagine how different kinds of people experience stuff so vividly that they can write about it like it was real? Seems like if you can do that when you're making up fiction, you ought to be able to do it in real life, too. Maybe I need to start living more like my whole life is a book.

Thursday, August 8

Things are slowly returning to normal at home, except for the absence of Charlotte's phone calls. My father made vegetarian tacos tonight—which I thought was a genuinely meaningful gesture—and he delivered a few lines in his damaged Mexican accent that the world affectionately recognizes as his trademark. My mother made a vague comment about the possibility of our all enrolling in a one-day intensive clog-dancing workshop. And the famous Summer Vacation List has appeared on the refrigerator. It happens pretty much like clockwork a few days before any Blennerhasset vacation, even an overnight, is planned. The list has different categories and we're all supposed to contribute to each one: "to pack," "to buy," and the always-popular "don't forget!"

I was surprised when I first saw it. I guess I've lost track of the time. August snuck in so quietly, it just doesn't feel like time for vacation. But the Blennerhassetts are champions of tradition, and the tradition sayeth that the 2nd and 3rd weeks in August are the days we spend at the la—

Oh, crap.

Insomnia.

1:17 a.m. Okay, I've double-checked my notebook entries and confirmed that Charles said they needed a place to stay for only two weeks. If they arrived the day after I gave Karma the key, according to my notebook, that would have put them in the lake house by Sunday, July 14. Two weeks from then would be Sunday, July 28. July 28 was the day Charles took me to the train station and I came home. Did he say anything about their leaving that day? I can't remember! They were probably leaving the next day. Right?

OPTIONS:

A) Assume two weeks is two weeks, and rest assured that even as I write this the LeBlancs have already cleared out of the lake house and left it immaculate, and that by the time the Blennerhasset family arrives on Sunday, August 11, there will be no trace whatsoever of them and no one will be the wiser for the whole very well intentioned episode.

B) Now that things have relaxed a bit in the Blennerhassett household, and after encouraging family enrollment in intensive clog-dancing workshop, I engage my parents in a mature conversation in which I mention having allowed the LeBlancs to stay at our lake house, using past-tense verbs to describe everything, and we all get a chuckle out of the whole thing with no harm ultimately done.

C) Like the characters in *Star Trek: Voyager*, I am sucked away by a tetryon beam that deposits me in the Delta Quadrant, a hundred thousand light-years from home.

All things considered, I think Option C may be my best bet.

3:00 a.m.

LIST OF THINGS I CANNOT DO:

1. I cannot go to the lake house to make sure the LeBlancs are out.
2. I cannot ask anyone else to go for me without giving the game away.
3. I cannot call the lake house, because the phone is not connected.
4. I cannot leave a message on the LeBlancs' home machine because the number is unlisted.
5. I cannot ask the smartest person I know, Charlotte McGrath, for advice, because I have wronged her and am not sure if she will still be my friend and plus she is not really speaking to me.
6. I cannot find a tetryon beam to transport me to the Delta Quadrant.

5:00 a.m.

LIST ADDENDUM:

7. I cannot sleep.

Friday, August 9
A place called Hope.

It was wrong, it was inappropriate, it was totally bogus for me to even think of asking for help after the way I've behaved to her. But I called Charlotte and told her the whole story with NO omissions, and begged for help. I told her that I'd spent days thinking about what she'd said, and how I'd even talked to my parents about it, and how right she'd been about some things. I told her I hadn't been treating her like the incredibly good friend she was, and I'd put her through a very unpleasant time, and how I was so sorry and wished I could take it back.

She didn't make it easy for me, but I guess she was entitled. She repeated most of the things she'd said during our last conversation, about how badly I'd behaved, and I said I was listening and I understood. Then she started in on the LeBlancs, and she said she needed me to understand that what they had done in allowing Lily Blennerhassett, technically a child, to give them access to her parents' vacation home, was inappropriate. Three days ago, F.B.s, I would have fought that tooth and nail, and said anything to defend the LeBlancs' honor. But I know enough now to realize that wasn't going to do me any good with Charlotte. And actually, something is starting to bother me: Why the LeBlancs didn't make sure to let me know WHAT DAY THEY WERE LEAVING, since I specifically told them we spend part of August in the house. Not to judge them or anything, because I know they are in the middle of a lot of important work. But they might have thought to settle that little detail. So I am willing to admit to Charlotte that the LeBlancs (EVEN the LeBlancs) are capable (though through minimal fault of their own) of behaving (in a very tiny way) inappropriately. I did not say the stuff in parentheses to Charlotte. For now I think it's enough that I'm beginning to understand that she is right about a lot of stuff.

She wasn't particularly sympathetic.

She wasn't all that friendly.

She wasn't in the mood for any small talk.

But she had four words for me, four words that ushered out the hovering cloud of doom and brought hope back into my life. And the words were:

FEDERAL EXPRESS, SATURDAY DELIVERY.

3:00 p.m. It is done. There are enough prevacation errands that needed doing to get my grounding temporarily lifted. It was simple. I wrote a quick note to the LeBlancs explaining that I was just confirming that they really had only needed the house for two weeks and were now gone (and therefore not reading the note!) but in the interests of specificity (MIRACULOUS word, F.B.s, and

SO much fun to say though it requires practice), I was reminding them of my family's arrival on Sunday and confirming that they needed to be out before our arrival, and that obviously it would be great to have everything looking exactly as they'd found it on arrival.

The Federal Express office was exactly where Charlotte said it was. And for the remains of my allowance plus a small loan from Charlotte, the Overnight Letter envelope addressed to The LeBlanc Family, c/o Blennerhassett, 6 Lake Road, Hamlette, N.Y., will be neatly delivered tomorrow by 1:35. I've therefore delivered the (probably unnecessary) alert to the LeBlancs, and I haven't had to break curfew or worry my friend and family in the process.

I do believe I may have judged this Young Executive Camp a little harshly.

Saturday, August 10

Good news and baddish news. The good news is I called FedEx and they confirmed my package was safely delivered. The baddish news is that the package was signed for by Charles LeBlanc. Meaning that as of 1:35 P.M. today, they were still at the lake house.

But I shouldn't worry. Obviously I made the right decision in going ahead and reminding them of the date, and after all the trouble Charles went to making sure my parents didn't know what was going on, the last thing he'd want to do was get caught in the house. Well, I don't mean caught, exactly. That sounds a little criminal. If I were writing on a laptop, I could just change that word immediately, instead of being stuck with my first choice (because crossing out looks too messy). Anyway, what I mean is I'm sure the last thing Charles wants is for my parents to know I let them stay there. So really, then, there ISN'T any bad news, the reminder has been received, and obviously they'll be gone by tonight, actually they're probably already gone, and all because I have a very good friend who is familiar with the workings of courier services that deliver Extremely Important Documents even on Saturdays.

I am a little confused about the LeBlancs, though. I'm not trying to say I don't realize how incredibly lucky I was to have them come into my life. I'm not trying to say they're not the most amazing people I've ever met. It's just that I did do them this favor, and even if it is the only truly good and selfless thing I've ever done and they've done millions of truly good and selfless things . . . I still think maybe they should have stayed only for the two weeks I said they could. That is all I'm saying.

I'm going to go and visit my friend Charlotte now.

Sunday, August 11
Backseat of the Honda.

10:45 a.m. All set to go. I'm even in the car a full fifteen minutes before departure time so that my father will not experience an Atmosphere of Rushing that could lead to loss of temper. The way my parents have ruthlessly packed the Honda with supplies, you'd think we were going off with Robert Falcon Scott for an eighteen-month expedition to reach the South Pole. Hamlette is less than a two-hour drive. But already this morning the car has been gassed, the tires pumped with air, the oil changed, the wiper fluid levels checked, and our cooler stuffed with representatives from every food group for Blennerhassetts who may become uncontrollably hungry en route. This in spite of the fact that every year, for even longer than we've been celebrating Dad's birthday at Szechuan House, we've been stopping at the Kingstorm McDonald's just off the ramp of Exit 72. It may seem to you, Future Biographers, that my parents can be logically assumed, with what scholars know about them, to be McDonald's haters. And I am pleased to confirm that for 364 days each year, they are. But on the first Sunday of the second week of August, every year, the contents of the cooler in the Honda are found to be inadequate in some way, and grumbling loudly, my father switches on the blinker and heads onto the ramp of Exit 72, doing exactly the speed limit.

Allow me to predict the immediate future, F.B.s. We will enter the McDonald's. My parents will stare up the menu with disapproving looks. They will sigh, and with greatly pained expressions they will both order Big Macs, and when the cashier asks if they'd like their orders supersized, they'll shrug their agreement in a way that makes it clear to everyone that they have accepted that resistance is futile.

Once seated, they will simultaneously bite into their Big Macs, each with one hand protectively resting on their carton of fries, and their faces will both take on the kind of rapt expression you see in an old-time painting of a girl who has just become possessed by the spirit of a loving and powerful angel who hovers just over her surrounded by beams of celestial light and glory.

There. Now I've saved the trouble of writing about it later, while it's happening, and getting ketchup on my journal.

1:50 p.m. Everything proceeding as predicted. My parents are practically glowing with post-McDonald's euphoria, burping and complaining about "that terrible food" and smiling at each other like honeymooners. Things are looking peaceful in Hamlette. We just passed the abandoned Esso station, no signs of any problems

THERE. Not that I'm expecting problems anywhere.

I can see our driveway ahead! Looks quite tidy. And . . .

YES! The LeBlancs' car is not in the driveway. Not that I was ever worried, Future Biographers. I had Federal Express on my side the whole time.

My parents are already out of the car, wrestling their suitcases toward the house. As I've repeatedly explained to them, a writer cannot be interrupted when she is in the middle of expressing a thought. If they would just give me a laptop, I might have finished getting it all down by now. But this longhand thing is slowing me down. The Honda is a very bumpy ride, after all.

So I'm just going to take my time here and finish recording what is obviously a very important moment in my life for the benefit of Future Biographers, whom I will not deny detailed information just because my parents have gone inside.

Yes, it's important for a Writer to Take Enough Time. It's pretty quiet up there at the house. I've rolled my window down, not because I'm trying to hear anything, but because it occurs to me that a nice fresh breeze might help to coax extra details for you F.B.s onto paper.

I do hear a little something, though, now that I've mentioned it. It's the sound of my father's voice. Raised. He's shouting something like "WHAT IN THE NAME OF SAM HILL HAPPENED IN HERE?"

That evening, darkish. I'm very busy lying facedown on my bed. I don't have much time to fritter away writing down a series of events that really, if you want my opinion, ought to be considered downright amusing by all involved. But this is a notebook, after all, not a novel. So I suppose the truth must be recorded.

It isn't as bad as it looks. I'm going to stick with that, in spite of my parents' reaction. It is not as bad as it looks. Most of the damage is removable. Any well-made scouring pad and bottle of bleach-enhanced cleanser could tell you that. The discerning consumer of today is also aware that many institutions have rug and upholstery steam-cleaning machines available for rental at quite reasonable rates. So really I feel that all that is required here is a little resourcefulness and some elbow grease. And, if they insist, an exterminator.

I'm going to argue that I think pesticides are a little over the top in this case. First of all, you can't blame the ants for coming inside in large numbers once word got out of the availability of leftover food on the kitchen surfaces. And though I'll admit that the startle factor takes some getting used to, some of the ants are downright cute if you look closely. It isn't as if they're cockroaches, for heaven's sake. I mean, we all remember that old song about "the ants go marching one by one," and let us not forget that the refrain is "Hurrah! Hurrah!" Not "eek" or "step on them," but "hurrah"! Ants as the subject of celebration and good cheer. I rest my case.

The bathtub situation, I admit, is going to be a little harder to fix. We've all always enjoyed the little built-in shelf unit over the tub. It's perfectly located and has enough generously sized shelves to hold representatives from all the soap and hair-care families. Plus hooks for loofahs, cups for razors and pumice foot scrubbers, and— Well. You get the picture. And it did look rather like a fallen hero, lying there at the bottom of the tub among the crumbs of caulking and shards of ceramic tile. I don't know if it can be fixed.

There, I've said it. I don't know if it can be fixed.

But the rest of the mess can be undone. With just a few days of good hard work, the house will look like its old self again. So I've got to repeat myself here and say that the damage really isn't as bad as it looks. What's been done to the house is forgivable. It's what's been done to me that is not.

Because in the midst of the mess, and the dirty dishes and the moldy bologna (which can't even be the LeBlancs' because they're vegetarians, right?) and the hardened crumbs and the petrified appetizers, in the midst of the scuffed floor and the smelly refrigerator and the sticky table, right smack in the center of the kitchen where it could hardly be missed by Helen Keller herself, lay an opened Federal Express envelope. My letter to the LeBlancs was lying open next to it. Signed in pen with my name, Lily Blennerhassett. And in under a minute of reading, my parents knew who was to blame for the condition of the lake house, and how they had come to be staying there in the first place.

Betrayal.

Later—how much later I'm not sure. I think I need to rescind the betrayal statement.

Because there could be an explanation. Okay, obviously the LeBlancs made a mistake somehow—they were still in the house when my FedEx came, and they realized they had to get out fast, so they couldn't really clean up properly. Or left a mess, or whatever. Maybe they didn't mean to leave my letter right out on the table where it would be found. Or maybe they thought it might be a growing experience for me if—if . . .

Monday, August 12
On my hands and knees.

I thought dishpan hands were just a made-up thing people tossed into conversation to be funny. Now that I have one attached to the end of each wrist, I'm not finding them so amusing. And unlike Oliver Twist, who made the mistake of asking for a second bowl of gruel at a pretty bad time, I left the topic of our lack of rubber housecleaning gloves alone.

I have scoured and scrubbed and mopped. I have wiped and rinsed and rubbed. I have pretreated, disinfected, and laundered. And I have not even finished half of it.

And the more I scrub, the more I start letting those words in, those words I wanted to rescind before, those words that describe the LeBlancs as people who maybe probably made a disgusting mess in our house maybe possibly on purpose and who maybe almost definitely left without caring or trying to clean it up and who maybe somewhat absolutely got me into Huge Huge Trouble for no apparent reason.

10:46 p.m. Addendum—Written with the Assistance of Roget and His Thesaurus:

Finks. Scoundrels. Villains. Blackguards. Miscreants. Wastrels. Wretches. Stinkers. Rotters. Blighters (British usage). Cads. Scapegraces.

You know, Future Biographers, to whom I refer.

Tuesday, August 13

I, Lily Blennerhassett, retract all comments both oral and written made with regard to the level of damage inflicted on the Blennerhassett lake house. I take it all back. Having personally cleaned most of the house, I can now say it was much, much worse than it looked.

Wednesday, August 14

When I was about seven or eight, I thought my grandfather was friends with Johann Sebastian Bach. I more than thought it. I actually remembered being at my grandfather's house one night when the famous composer came by to visit. And I always told the story with a bit of regret (as much regret as an eight-year-old can throw into her voice), because while Grandaddy and the famous composer had coffee downstairs, I remained upstairs in bed. Simply too tired to get up and go down and say hi. It always bothered me that I missed my chance to say hello to that world-famous man.

It wasn't until about two years ago that it occurred to me it hadn't been Johann Sebastian Bach downstairs with my grandfather. A quick peek in the B section of the *Concise Oxford Dictionary of Music* confirmed it—the great man of classical music died in 1750. And you can't blame my grandfather for this little misunderstanding. He never said anything about knowing Bach, though he did have a friend named John Sebastian. The Bach thing was just something I absorbed somehow, the way you absorb the fact that your sister is prettier than you, or your house is a little fancier than your best friend's. But it was ridiculous, and it wasn't real, and now that I'm older and wiser I can see that.

Tell me, Future Biographers, what other conclusion is there? The LeBlancs cared about keeping their stay at the lake house a secret only WHILE THEY WERE HERE. Once they left, they didn't care who knew about it. In fact, they seem to have gone out of their way to let my parents know what I'd done.

Does anyone REALLY know who their friends are?

Thursday, August 15
In the doghouse.

I have progressed beyond grounding. I have been punished so thoroughly and painfully that I will probably never recover. My parents chose not to penalize financially, to imprison, or to thwack me. They chose, instead, to tell me some Ugly Truths.

A Little Devastating Conversation:

ME: I know, I know everything you're going to say.
DAD: I don't think you do, Lily.
ME: I do, though, and go ahead and say it because I deserve everything you're going to say and do, but I just want to tell you that I'm sorry. I had no idea . . . I just thought it would be nice . . .
MOM: Lily, you need to know some things.
ME: No, I know that. I'm just saying I thought it was the right thing to do, because they didn't have anyplace to go during the tests.
DAD: The tests?
ME: The environmental testing they were allowing on their property. It wasn't safe for them to be around, so they were supposed to leave for two weeks, and they were all set to go to a hotel, but that would have cost money

184

that could have gone to Hug the Planet.

MOM: Hug the Planet?

ME: The environmental watchdog group that they founded. They never asked me anything, I swear, about staying at the house. But when Charles started talking about how they were going to have to take HTP money for this hotel, and Veronique had said something about people's vacation homes being empty when there are home-less—when there are people who need a place to stay—

(I know. I know. After everything, it seems like I'm still defending them. Actually, I'm defending ME, and this is my way of doing it. Anyway, all this stuff is true. It's important not to forget the good stuff the LeBlancs were trying to do.)

DAD: Lily—

ME: I just offered it. I didn't think it would do any harm. And Charles said he knew you didn't like them and he kept refusing!

DAD: Lily—

ME: He kept refusing, don't you see? But I kept insisting, and finally he accepted on the condition I didn't tell you guys, because he said he didn't want my generous action to get me into trouble.

MOM: Oh, dear. Oh, Lily.

ME: I AM sorry.

DAD: Lily, do you think it is YOU we're angry at?

ME: Uhh . . . yes?

MOM: We're not happy with what you did, honey. But you are not the only one who has behaved badly. They are. They took a calculated advantage of you. They did a real number on you. They deliberately manipulated you.

ME: Aren't you listening to me? I TOLD you! I had to practically beg Charles to accept my offer.

DAD: He knew what he was doing.

ME: But—

DAD *(in a tone that automatically strips me of the ability to interrupt)*: Lily. There are some things you need to know about these people. Things that, had we told you to start with, might have prevented all of this.

(No actual words from me, just a worried, questioning look.)

DAD: I'm not even sure where to begin.

MOM: How about their names?

DAD: Right. Charlie and Vera White. Those are the LeBlancs' real names. Charlie and Vera White. And their daughter's name is Kay.

(Pause. I swallow deeply. This might not be true. They could be wrong. And even if they're not, what's in a name? So maybe they didn't end up with the same names they started off with. Is that a crime?)

MOM: Charlie and Vera White became Charles and Veronique LeBlanc about nine years ago. Around the same time they ran into their first major money problems. They just overspent. They tried to embrace a lifestyle they couldn't afford. We used to see them occasionally at the holidays—Vera was always in a designer dress, the very latest and hippest, and she had very expensive tastes in jewelry.

DAD: So did Charlie. And they were always jetting off somewhere—

MOM: Or saying they were—

DAD: To Aspen, Monaco, Paris. Whatever was the flashiest.

MOM: The ritziest.

> *(Lies. LIES! Who are my parents to judge the LeBlancs' clothes and vacation spots? Just because they don't understand anything trendy. Just because they are not part of the twenty-first century!)*

MOM: If they were so involved with giving everything to their environmental interests, Lily, didn't it strike you odd that they wore expensive clothes and had such a splashy car?

> *(Well, they—if you consider that—I don't—well, yes. That does seem a little odd.)*

DAD: Charlie had some money of his own to start, actually. His parents had left him a nice bundle. If he'd invested it, they could have lived very well off of it and eventually provided for their daughter with a trust fund.

But Charlie went straight out and got a fancy sports car and rented a house in the glitziest neighborhood in town.

(I am now actively trying not to listen. Because it's starting to sound like the truth, and I just don't want any more of it right now. I can't actually put my fingers in my ears. That wouldn't go over. But I'm mentally reciting presidents in sequence, starting with George Washington.)

MOM: And it wasn't long before the money was gone. So they had to start looking for more.

DAD: And they started with their family.

(John Adams.)

DAD: First they just out-and-out asked for loans. From Charlie's sisters, from his grandmother, from Vera's mother.

MOM: But they never paid the loans back. Never even tried. Family is family. They talk to one another. We all started hearing things.

(Thomas Jefferson.)

DAD: That's when they started getting downright dishonest.

(James Madison. James Monroe.)

DAD: Charlie started hounding the cousins with these great investment opportunities he said he had.

MOM: He'd even produce literature about the companies, Len, remember?

(John Quincy Adams. Andrew Jackson.)

DAD: Yes, he did very thorough work. And the thing is,

Lily, and this is what is important for you to understand, the guy is a genius at fooling people. As a con man, he's unbelievably talented. He talked scores of perfectly sensible people into handing over their money, no questions asked. He always made them feel smart, and involved, and honored to have been singled out to join their "team," as he called it.

(Who comes after Jackson? WHO FLIPPING COMES AFTER JACKSON?)

MOM: But no matter how much they were taking in, they were spending more. I remember Delia's mother saying that at one point they had over thirty credit cards between them, all in different names, all maxed out.

(THERE'S A WHOLE STRETCH OF UNRE-MEMBERABLE PRESIDENTS HERE!!)

DAD: Their creditors were constantly after them, so they were always moving. That poor girl Kay never stayed in the same school more than six months. Then she began to get into trouble, playing hooky. Shoplifting.

(Lincoln. I'll just skip to Lincoln. ABRAHAM LIN-COLN!)

MOM: We hadn't heard anything about them for a few years. I expect it was because they ran out of family members who hadn't already been burned, or at least heard enough to know better. They must have moved on to complete strangers.

(Andrew Johnson. Ulysses S. Grant.)

DAD: And then they met you. You were young, impressionable, maybe a little bored without Charlotte—

(*Roosevelts, Teddy and Franklin! HARRY TRUMAN! JFK!*)

DAD: And they got their hooks into you.

(*Niiiiiiiiiiiiiixxxxxxxooooooooooonnnnnnnn!!!!!!!*)

DAD: I can picture it all. Hanging out with you, making you feel important, making you feel special and, what do you call it, cool?

(*I am out of presidents. I am close to throwing up.*
Why won't they stop talking?)

MOM: Probably throwing in a few personal questions every once in a while about how we lived, whether we had more than one house.

(*If I threw up right now, they might stop talking.*)

DAD: Lily? You haven't said anything.

(*Bill Clinton.*)

MOM: Honey? I know this is very upsetting to you. These are not decent people.

ME (*unable to contain myself*): What about Hug the Planet? What about all their environmental work?

DAD: Sweetheart, I'd be willing to bet a year's pay that there is no Hug the Planet.

ME: But I've been there! To the office! In an apartment on Main Street right in town.

MOM: That's where their last home address was, Lily.

They probably lived there.

ME: I saw literature. Brochures. They gave them to me.

DAD: Hug the Planet sounds like Charlie's latest money-making venture. If you print up a nice brochure with a color logo and some politically correct statements, a lot of people will actually give you money. But unless Charlie has become a completely different person in the past few years, he kept that money for himself.

ME: I— Maybe— You can't actually know . . . Why did you wait all this time to bring this up?

MOM: We didn't think it was that important. We didn't like or trust the Whites, and we knew to steer clear of them, but we could see you were fascinated by them. I made sure you knew I didn't want you around them. I didn't think I needed to take it any further than that. None of us ever thought that even Charlie White would sink low enough to con a child.

(Is that what I was doing all that time I was so happy? Being conned?)

DAD: We didn't think your sitting with them at one lousy reception would do any harm. We thought once the wedding was over, we'd have seen the last of them. Never underestimate Charlie White.

ME: I'm . . . feeling a little sick.

MOM: This is a lot for you to take in. But we wanted to make sure you knew the whole story. You did do something wrong, Lily, in offering our home to people you really didn't know and not telling us about it. But the point is, Charlie and Vera have fooled people far older and more worldly than you. I wish it hadn't happened. I wish I had treated you like an adult and just told you the whole story up front. And yes, I do wish you hadn't asked those people to stay here. But I can't say I really blame you for it.

DAD: And ultimately, not much harm has been done. They left a monumental mess—

MOM: I've never seen such filth—how did they do it in such a short period of time?

DAD: —but you've done a fine job cleaning it, Lily, so I think we're even. It's not like Charlie swindled us out of our life's savings, after all. I can put this in perspective and feel grateful the damage was as minimal as a trashed house.

ME *(eyes welling with unsummoned tears)*: I'm sorry.
(Family hug.)

ME: Can I go to my room? I kind of need to write all this down.

MOM: Of course you can, sweetheart.

And so that brings us to now. I'm not stupid. I know the ring of truth when I hear it. I know my parents wouldn't talk that way about anyone unless they were certain of their facts. The LeBlancs I thought I knew would never have gotten me in trouble on purpose. But the Whites would.

It was all a lie. A vaudeville show starring Yours Truly, Lily Blennerhassett. It was all a con game. A three-dimensional work of fiction. Except for one thing—they *are* family. And that makes it worse.

Friday, August 16

I am an idiot.

Saturday, August 17

Mom is trying to get me excited about the oven-mitt–making craft set she brought. But I don't feel creative. I don't feel interested in anything. All I can think about is the LeB—the Whites. Things just keep coming to me.

The HTP credit card being rejected. Me ending up buying Karma that stuff. (And what will I do when the bill comes?) The earrings Karma got me—did she shoplift them? Kayma, Kar, whatever she is, meeting me in the coffee shop. I'm such a loser—I was so psyched about seeing her! And once she had the key to the lake house, she couldn't get away from me fast enough.

They made me sleep on the porch. On the PORCH! In my own house! And I smiled and said that was GREAT!

See, the worst thing isn't finding out that the LeBlancs (Whites) are con artists. The worst thing is that now I can't even look back on how happy I was when I was with them, when Karma was my friend, because it turns out it wasn't real. It was all made up, on purpose, to fool me. If I could feel like it was worth it, because I had such a great time while I had Karma and her family to hang out with, I could live with that.

But my grandfather did not know Johann Sebastian

Bach, and Karma LeBlanc and her parents did not like me.

11:58 p.m. I have decided I am too gullible to be a writer.

Sunday, August 18

I will be an accountant, like my father, and carry on the family tradition. And one day, maybe, all this will be forgotten.

My only consolation is it can't get any worse.

Monday, August 19

My dad was playing "Where Have All the Flowers Gone" on his piccolo while Mom and I finished a jigsaw puzzle of a basket full of kittens after assembling our macramé plant holders. All was as it should be in the Blennerhassett lake house. I picked up my notebook, because even though I know I can no longer be a writer (because I am too naïve), I do feel an obligation to finish the story (and get that Advanced English credit). So here's what's just happened.

There was a knock on the door, and we were all surprised because we never get any visitors at the lake house except for the Whittakers, and they ALWAYS call first. So I had a brief, terrifying moment thinking that when Dad opened the door, he would find Charlie and Vera, complete with knockoff Louis Vuitton luggage, standing at the door and beaming. But when Dad actually opened the door, there was a man standing there I didn't recognize. All he said was "Leonard A. Blennerhassett?" Dad nodded. And the guy just handed him an envelope and walked away without waiting for him to open it or anything. That's what just happened.

Maybe it's a prize of some kind. A cash award. Sweepstakes winnings. But where are the roses? Where are the cameras and the spokesperson?

4:48 p.m. Dad is opening the envelope. Doesn't look

like a prize. So that's a disappointment. Dad's mouth is dropping open.

4:49 p.m. Dad has dropped the envelope and its contents on the floor.

4:50 p.m. Dad is making himself a gimlet.

4:55 p.m. Dad has wandered onto the front porch with his gimlet. He has not spoken. My mother followed him out, put a questioning hand on his shoulder. The envelope and paper are still on the floor.

5:00 p.m. I'm going to go have a look, Future Biographers. (Though I realize now there will be no Future Biographies of me since I'm going to be an accountant, it is hard for me to stop addressing you by name because I've grown rather fond of you.)

5:04 p.m. I'm not exactly sure what it is, but I know it isn't good. Across the top of the paper it says SUMMONS. And it starts off (and I'm copying here, hoping there's no copyright infringement taking place) "You are hereby summoned to answer this Complaint in this action and to serve a copy of your Answer, or if the Complaint is not served with this Summons, to serve a Notice of Appearance, on the plaintiff's attorney, within twenty days …" And it goes on like that for a long time, in a really appalling run-on sentence . . . and there are some names and things at the top and bottom . . . .

Good grief. Charlie and Vera White are suing us.

Tuesday, August 20
Unexpectedly home from vacation.

The first thing we did was pack up and come home immediately. We sailed past the Kingstorm McDonald's like it was a leaking nuclear power plant. I tell you In Strict Confidence that we exceeded the speed limit on three occasions. When we got home, Dad got on the phone, and he's been on it ever since.

My parents gave it to me straight, and I'll give it to you straight. Apparently (allegedly?) at our lake house the shower shelf fell when Vera, while washing her hair, slipped in the tub. Allegedly (apparently?) she grabbed at the shelf and it pulled out and Vera and shelf tumbled down. In addition to some bumps and scrapes (they call them contusions—not a bad word), Vera reportedly experienced a level of trauma and stress so significant that she has not yet recovered from it. This, according to her claim, has prevented her from functioning normally, not the least because she has now developed a phobia of tubs and is unable to bathe in a normal fashion, which is causing her to suffer socially as well as professionally (I don't remember her HAVING a job), and this is all due to gross negligence on the part of my parents, who showed a complete and reckless disregard for the safety of others when they neglected to put those little nonslip strips in the tub in the first place. So the onset of this phobia is being blamed on my parents by way of a lawsuit. And that lawsuit has placed a dollar value on the phobic and unwashed Vera, to the tune of $1.6 million.

I have destroyed the Blennerhassetts.

Insomnia.

1:18 a.m. I know something about phobias myself. My mom has one. No one in the immediate Blennerhassett family ever fully recovered from it. When I was about eight, I went on this pony ride at a local fair, and having a safety-minded mother, I was made to wear this smelly riding helmet they kept at the ticket booth. Probably a hundred kids had worn it already that morning. I still remember how it felt—like a bowl of lukewarm applesauce on my head.

A few weeks later, my head started itching. My mother took me to the doctor, who backed three feet away before informing my mom that I'd gotten head lice. I will never forget the look on my mother's face. You'd have thought she had looked into the sky and seen a massive comet hurtling toward the earth. And because she'd spent a significant amount of time snuggling head to head with me while reading Laura Ingalls Wilder books to me at bedtime, she asked the doctor to look at her head. And, well. She had head lice, too.

It was on the way to the drugstore to get the lice shampoo that we got pulled over. She really was driving like a maniac, weaving all over the place trying to steer and swat at her head at the same time. It was the only time she ever got pulled over by the police. I'll never forget the officer tapping on the window and saying, "How are we doing today?" My mother responded by bursting into tears and shrieking, "WE HAVE LICE!" We were let go without a ticket.

I have to stress at this point that Charlotte stood by me during that, the at-the-time worst thing that had ever happened to me. She came over, and sat in chairs I'd sat in, and hugged me, and plopped down right next to me to watch TV, even though she might have gotten my lice from doing any of those things. She didn't get grossed out when I scratched my head so hard, you could have heard it in Delaware. She kept me company while I had the lice shampoo soaking on my head for ten minutes. She was a champion.

The next few days were filled with laundering, vacuuming, lathering up with the lice shampoo, and the worst part—having my hair combed through with the tiny comb you use to get the stinkers out of your hair. My father combed my mother's hair for her. And the whole time, and this was days and days, she was in this controlled state of hysteria, like every second it was a massive effort for her not to break out screaming, "Get them off me! Get them off me!" She never completely got over it.

To this day, Mom's face turns ashen if I so much as

scratch the top of my head. A few months ago we pulled into the parking lot of a convenience store, and my mother screamed and pointed at a sign. The sign said WE HAVE ICE. She had just misread it. And even though we concluded it really was just ice the store had, she still wouldn't go in. Just in case it was a misprint and the sign really was meant to say WE HAVE LICE.

I know this is a long story to go into for someone who is going to be an accountant, not a writer. But I am simply trying to point out that my mother suffers from a Real and Legitimate Phobia. But did it ever occur to her to file a lawsuit against the managers of the pony ride? To ruthlessly go after their family's life's savings? No. Did she ever consider that these people should in some way be held responsible for the disruption of our household because of their bug-filled riding helmet? No. Did she ever feel entitled to some kind of cash payment because in the course of life something unpleasant happened to our family through no fault of our own? No. Because unlike some people, my mother understands that things happen to a person in life, and you deal with it, and you go on about your business. You do not abuse the legal system and persecute people with ridiculous lawsuits for free money. My mother is a model citizen. I only hope someday I can live up to her standard.

I HATE the LeBlancs.

Wednesday, August 21

Nothing concrete seems to be happening. Dad makes calls to people who aren't at their desks, and his messages don't get returned. The waiting is agony. Especially for me (the one person who has NO right to complain) because I know, in spite of what my parents said, that this is my fault. I'm so, so scared. Do Mom and Dad even have $1.6 million? Can someone really take all their savings away from them? Can a judge somewhere plunk his gavel down and order them to get out their checkbook?

I just don't understand. My dad has worked hard his whole life slogging away behind a desk wearing a suit and tie and helping other people manage their money. He's put away a college fund for me, he got us our lake house, he keeps us going. Charlie, on the other hand, has spent his life bumming around and mooching, stealing even, from other people. Can he really waltz in now and take everything my dad has worked for? All the money? The houses?

What have I done?

Insomnia.

1:14 a.m. I've been going through my things, trying to figure out what I can sell. I wonder if I could get anything for the shiny green dress. It's only been worn once. I've just been thinking, if I could have some kind of tag sale or something, maybe I could help raise money. Wait, though. Would Charlie just get *that* money, too?

Nobody I know has $1.6 million lying around. Dad is going to have to sell our house. Where are we going to go? Will they take the car, too, or can we live in that? Will I have to switch schools? Will I ever go to college with no money to pay for it? Can you BE an accountant without going to college?

1:25 a.m. I'VE JUST READ WHAT I'VE WRITTEN! Still, after everything I've done, all I'm doing is worrying about myself! I HAVE RUINED MY FAMILY! In one single, breathtakingly stupid action, I have bankrupted them! My father will be working overtime until he's 90. My mother will never be able to afford another clog-dancing workshop. They're going to lose everything. Everything.

I hate myself.

Thursday, August 22

Charlotte has descended upon me like a corporate Robin Hood emerging from the Sherwood Forest Office Park with her band of Merry Businessmen. I called her when I got back from the lake house to say hi, but I didn't tell her about the trashing of the lake house and the lawsuit. She was right about the LeBlancs. They were Criminal People. She was right, but I just couldn't bear to tell her about it. My parents must have told her parents.

I feel really stupid and ashamed and embarrassed. But the minute I set eyes on Charlotte, I realized I'd never been happier to see her in my life. Maybe she could make some sense out of all this mess. Maybe she knew someone from Young Executive Camp who could help.

"First of all," Charlotte is saying as she paces furiously back and forth in my bedroom, "your parents are right when they say you do not bear all of the blame here. You've been hoodwinked by a family of professional posers. I say there's some HONOR in that."

Really, Charlotte can be very, very nice.

"It's disgusting!" Charlotte continues. "A blatant abuse of our legal system—a slap in the face of our Founding Fathers—graffiti on the Constitution!"

Yeah.

"And these 1-800-LAWSUIT firms enabling idiots like the LeBlancs—"

"Whites," I correct firmly.

"—the LeWhites to bog down the system and threaten the very foundation of freedom our country was founded on!"

Yeah.

"There ought to be serious penalties a person faces when they manipulate a system designed to protect people and twist it for their own financial benefit! They should stand to lose everything themselves!"

Yeah.

"But Char," I say, taking advantage of a brief pause to introduce the subject pressing most heavily on me. "What about the money? What if Charlie and Vera actually win this lawsuit—what will happen to us? Can they really make Dad pay them one point six million dollars? We'll be bankrupted! We'll have to go on welfare. Oh my god, can you even QUALIFY for welfare if you've lost your money in a lawsuit?"

Charlotte stops pacing and looks as me like she's just seen a hamster trying to operate a forklift.

"Lily, is THAT what's worrying you? Don't you know anything about insurance?"

Insurance? Don't you have to die to get that? Now I FEEL like a hamster trying to operate a forklift. I know I am out of my league, so I just sit quietly and wait.

Charlotte allows herself a moment of disappointment in my lack of knowledge, like a Jedi Master whose student has just cut off his own foot with his light saber.

"I do wish you'd read *The Economist* when I give it to you." She sighed. "Anyway. Insurance. If for some ridiculous and diabolical reason the LeWhites actually win this lawsuit, your parents won't actually have to pay the money out of their pockets. The insurance company will pay."

Insurance company? Insurance company? Who are these people, other than my new Very Good Friends?

"It's just like the hotel you stayed at. Remember I explained how their insurance rates went up because of frivolous lawsuits? Families have insurance, too, if they're sensible people. And your parents are the most sensible people I know."

She gives me a little look to indicate that in this case, the apple may have fallen a mile or two from the tree.

"You mean like health insurance?" I ask, eager to show I can at least use the word in a sentence.

"All kinds. Health, life, car. And liability insurance. In this pathetic day and age, you have to have it. Health insurance for your doctors' bills, car insurance if you smash the Honda. Homeowner's insurance if your house burns or floods. And liability insurance if a pair of twerps in knockoff designer clothes and fake French names slip in your bathtub and sue you."

The relief I feel is so overwhelming, I almost shout. But I need to be careful. This sounds too good to be true.

"So you're saying my parents aren't in danger of having to come up with one point six million dollars for Charlie and Vera?"

"Not if they have liability insurance, they aren't," Charlotte responded.

I'm sorry, but at this point I scream with joy.

"That's fabulous!" I yell.

"But it isn't!" Charlotte yells back. Charlotte rarely yells. "It's part of the whole problem. The sleazy lawyers encouraging people like the LeWhites to sue justify themselves by saying it's the insurance companies paying, so no one is really getting hurt. And the insurance companies don't want to be going to court all the time, so they agree on out-of-court settlements and fork over a smaller amount of money. Then the sleazy lawyer gets his thirty-three percent and the LeWhites get the rest and everybody's insurance rates go up to pay for it and the system keeps getting abused AND NO ONE IS DOING ANYTHING TO STOP IT! AND THAT IS NOT FABULOUS!"

I have listened to what Charlotte is saying, and I see that she is right, and that this is a bad thing, and that it has to be stopped before our world unravels into chaos. But inwardly, I can't help feeling gleeful.

We won't have to go on welfare.

Friday, August 23

After giving up on the lawyer who wasn't returning his phone calls, Dad apparently had a brainstorm and found another lawyer who was much more receptive. The lawyer is actually coming here today (a house call!) with some initial documents. I guess that's one thing Charlotte forgot to mention. That for every sleazy, bogus lawyer convincing people to sue the world so they can make a quick buck, there are also nice, decent lawyers trying to help out people in need. I imagine them all gathered somewhere, some kind of cruise ship or island equipped with loudspeakers, waiting for the next call to go out that an Innocent Party Has Been Wronged. Then they toss their briefcase into their rubber dinghy and sail briskly forth in the Name of Justice.

Well. Maybe not.

3:00 p.m. Excuse the clichéd ravings of a future accountant, but you could have knocked me down with a feather. In fact, I might have appreciated it.

The doorbell rang at more or less the right time of the lawyer's appointment. Dad had gone upstairs to look for something, and Mom was doing a little last-minute dusting (because, as we all know, no lawyer in his right mind will represent anyone who can't keep a sideboard properly buffed), so I went ahead and opened the door.

It was Delia.

I wasn't sure what I ought to say. Obviously, the timing was pretty bad. Not to mention being a little heavy in the irony section. Since I had met THEM at Delia's wedding and everything. Anyway, it wasn't a good time for a visit. There was serious work to be done. Insurance companies to be called. We certainly couldn't have Delia hanging about, refusing snacks and fainting on the furniture.

"Hi, Lily," Delia said. "Is your dad home?"

"No," I said quickly, without thinking. Then regretted it. Had I not lied ENOUGH? "Yes," I added.

Delia looked a little irritated.

"It's just not a great time," I said. "Maybe tomorrow?"

"I have an appointment," Delia said. And she actually folded her arms and tapped her foot. She was wearing a pretty fancy suit. Next to her tapping foot was a briefcase.

My mouth might have dropped open a tiny bit. Was DELIA our lawyer? Delia took a step back, like I might be thinking about biting her. Before either of us could think of anything to say, my dad walked up behind us.

"Delia," he said, gesturing for her to come in. "Thank you so much for coming. I don't know why I didn't think to call you in the first place."

"The pleasure is all mine," Delia said, brushing by me quickly. "I feel responsible for this, having invited them to the wedding. Ned tried to talk me out of it, but I had this ridiculous idea of family togetherness. *Mea culpa. Mea maxima culpa.*"

"What?" I asked. I hadn't actually meant to speak.

"It means the fault is mine—the fault is greatly mine."

(What is that, Latin? Can an accountant use that?)

Delia sat down on the couch and took off her jacket. Her arms were like pencils. I decided if she were a character in a Roald Dahl novel, her name would be Vanessa Lunchmaggot, and she would be wily and cunning.

She was taking some papers from her briefcase. My mother came in, and she and my father sat down next to Delia, and I couldn't help noticing the worried look around their eyes. I felt that awful guilty feeling again. Even if we weren't going on welfare, I had put my parents into an awful situation. They'd have to pay legal fees. Their insurance premiums were going to get more expensive. I hung my head a little and started to walk out.

"Lily?" Delia called. "I think you ought to stick around, if it's okay with you, Lenny. You're going to need to be in on this process, and at some point I'm going to need your help."

I probably looked as surprised as I felt. I thought I was in disgrace here. But I looked from Delia to Dad, and he nodded. So I sat down next to him.

"I've got some ideas," Delia began, "and I think you're

going to like them. And I've got to say it will be worth every penny I spent on law school to personally go after Charlie and Vera, after all the crap they've pulled. I must have been crazy to invite them to the wedding after everything they've done—it had just been so many years since they tried one of their stunts, I didn't think it would matter. You know how wedding lists go—if you don't invite one part of the family, you can't invite any of them. But oh, I could kick myself! Do you know Charlie 'borrowed' almost every penny in my great-aunt Kathleen's retirement account and never even tried to pay it back? A seventy-five-year-old lady who saved her salary from teaching first grade for fifty years! Left with nothing because she trusted her charming great-nephew! It makes me so mad, I could holler! So what do you say, Blennerhassetts? Let's you and I nail those weasels!"

VANESSA LUNCHMAGGOT TO THE RESCUE!

Sunday, August 25

I didn't exactly understand the legal precedents and potential actions Delia went through. But I didn't have to. The fury of this skinny woman, F.B.s! The vengeful intent! The focus! From what I can see, Delia is a woman to be taken very seriously. I misjudged her. Badly misjudged her. Why do I always do that? I look at someone and I immediately think I know everything I need to about them. *Mea culpa. Mea maxima culpa.*

In the meantime, it looks like more waiting. And though Delia has confirmed that my parents' liability insurance is entirely in order, and we should not be losing our house and living out of our car, I am still worried. Mom says I should try to distract myself. She even took me to the bookstore, the world's greatest place. She said I should try to read, get my mind off things.

The sky is practically black and the rain is pouring down. Usually the kind of weather I really enjoy. Housebound and book- and pen-bound. If I were the main character in a book by Richard Peck, maybe, or C. S. Lewis, this is the sort of weather that would lead me to the hidden time portal in the farthest recesses of the armor room, or to the dusty attic where I would encounter the ghost of a centuries-dead girl who bears an eerie resemblance to me. Or, perched in the window seat of a quiet and unused room on the top floor of a rented cottage, I would catch sight of a dim figure beckoning to me from the forest. Or, coming up the stairs, I would discover a loose floorboard covering a hole in which is hidden an old worn box, which is opened to reveal an antique oddly fashioned ceramic doll that exerts a strange power over me. Yes, the possibilities are endless for a main character stuck in a house on a black, rainy day.

I guess, depending on how you look at it, my summer could be a kind of book. Girl who wants to be writer and thinks boring parents are stifling her meets fascinating hip family and defies parents by hanging out with them, ultimately throwing her life into chaos and threatening everything she holds dear. I would read that book. I might have even written it, before I changed to being an accountant. It's too bad. It might have been a great book. I could have called it *Lily B. on the Brink of Cool*. Since I came so close. But that dream is all gone now.

Monday, August 26
Dress Barn. Back-to-School section dressing room.

I can't believe it was so easy. If only I'd known. All these years. I endured the first three shirts my mother brought in for me to try on, because I thought that is what a dutiful, repentant daughter ought to do. But when she appeared with the fourth consecutive high-necked, ruffly, lacy shirt, I took a deep breath and explained calmly that I really didn't think that style was flattering on me, and that I found it uncomfortable to wear. And she turned around, Future Biographers (or should I be including Future Accountants now?), and took it away. And when she came back, she had a dark-green cotton shirt with three buttons on the top, a scoop neck, and three-quarter-length sleeves. I loved it! We bought the shirt.

This truth thing is really, really good.

4:30 p.m. Just as I was beginning to feel a little better about life. But I can't write about it yet.

5:20 p.m. Not yet.

6:15 p.m. No.

8:40 p.m. It was after we bought the shirt. Mom had wandered away to the ruffled button-down section for old times' sake. And that's when it happened. I saw Karma. Kay. I saw Kay.

And she saw me.

She looked surprised. She looked uncomfortable. There was this moment. And then she kind of smiled, a small, superior smile. And I knew what she was thinking. She was thinking that, unfortunate as it was to see Lily Blennerhassett, it was no big deal. Because Lily Blennerhassett would never have the nerve to walk over and confront her. And maybe she was right. Lily Blennerhassett, writer, friend, and admirer of the LeBlancs, would not have confronted one of them face-to-face.

But Lily Blennerhassett, accountant, could.

I reached her in about twenty large steps.

"Lily," she said in greeting, trying to look nonchalant and not making eye contact at the same time.

"Kaaaay," I replied, and was rewarded by her slight wince. Her expression turned unpleasant. I knew everything, and she knew that I knew.

"Your mother off picking out some granny clothes for you?" she asked, tossing her hair.

"Stolen anything cute lately?" I shot back.

"What-E," she said. "I'm sure your parents have been feeding you a lot of sanctimonious and small-minded crap about me."

"While your parents are off running a scam at an old folks' home?" I shot back. Where do accountants get this stuff? It must come from the nerves they develop doing audits. Kay stared at me for a minute.

"I don't get involved in my parents' business," she said.

She shifted her weight from one foot to the other and looked at her watch, like the bus was twenty minutes late.

"You call what your parents do 'business'?" I asked.

"What else?" she replied, trying to look bored.

"I know a good lawyer who calls it grand larceny," I replied. (I sort of made that up on the spot.) And all the Karma suddenly went out of her face, and she was just nervous Kay for a moment.

Then she put her Karma face back on, tossing her hair over her shoulders.

"Oh, right, you're Little Miss Writer the Smart, I forgot. Smart enough to hand over the keys to your lake house behind your parents' back to people you barely knew."

Okay, that stung.

"Yes, the lake house," I said. "I need to ask you about that. There's just something I'd really like to know."

"What?" Kay said, looking irritated and anxious to walk away.

"Whatever the circumstances, I tried to do your family a favor. I got myself in a lot of trouble doing it. And you took my favor, and you thanked me by trashing the house and leaving my letter in the middle of the kitchen table so my parents would know what I had done the minute they walked in the door."

"So?"

"So, why? You got what you wanted. You got your free

place to stay. You got what you wanted out of me. Why finish it in such a mean way? Why go to the trouble of making sure I got punished for helping you out?"

There was a long silence.

"I have no idea what you're talking about," Kay said finally. "You're the one who got busted. This isn't my problem."

"Isn't your problem?" I asked, incredulous. "Hello? Is my universal translator off-line? Because I don't think you're hearing me."

"That's because you don't have anything to say that makes sense," Kay snapped. "You're Lenny and Phyllis's daughter, all right. You have all the personality of *Ladies' Home Journal.* I'm out of here."

That was it then. Kay wasn't going to face the truth, she was going to pretend it didn't exist.

And she stormed off, with her hair streaming behind her, which I used to think looked cool but now only made me notice she had bad posture. I watched her slouch away until I couldn't see anymore. I didn't seem to be feeling anything at all while I watched her. I didn't feel anything but what she had said—that I'm Lenny and Phyllis Blennerhassett's daughter, all right. And all I could think was that maybe she could have stood for a little Lenny and Phyllis in her life. It might have helped.

But I guess we'll never know.

Tuesday, August 27

It's still raining. And still no word from Delia on how things look, and what to expect next. The suspense is pretty hard to take. Mom and Dad seem calm one minute, anxious the next.

I'm curled up in my vintage seventies beanbag chair watching the rain come down. Maybe it will wash Charlie and Vera White clean off the face of the earth. But I suppose, once the sun finally came out, that two more finks would just sprout in their place.

I had just finished reading William Sleator's *Interstellar Pig* (vastly satisfying, F.B.s), and I felt like reading something else. But I was very comfortable and didn't want to get up, and the only other thing within reach was this. *Lily B. on the Brink of Cool.*. So I turned to the first page, and I started to read. I read straight through to the part about seeing Kay at the mall. And I was surprised.

My life is a novel. As I look back and read it over, I can see all the warning signs in my notebook, as clear as day. From the very first pages. It's like the Writer Me knew the LeBlancs were hosing me, even if the Me Me didn't. Now that I know who and what the Whites are, I can see it from the first moment I met them. I can sense the trouble coming. I see foreshadowing and character development. Suspense and pacing. I can see where Lily, where I, went

220

wrong. I can see how I judged people and things by their outward appearance and didn't scratch the surface enough to get the truth. My life is a novel. Would it make a difference to readers to know that it is all true, that it all happened just as I've said, or does it matter? Would Future Editors put notes in the margin about my mother, saying, "This character is not believable—no one would really want to attend an exhibition of Turn of the Century Earthenware"? Will truth always be stranger than fiction?

There I was, complaining from the very first page about waiting for Experience so I could begin my writing career. And little did I know I'd already started it. So with the greatest admiration and respect to all in the accounting profession, I think I have to change my mind about my future. I am no longer planning to become an accountant. And I'm not working on becoming a writer. I already AM one.

All I need now is an ending.

Wednesday, August 28

The deposition is going to be tomorrow. It's a big legal thingy, F.B.s, where you tell your side of the story and swear that it is the truth. I'm going to have to do most of the talking. I'm ready.

Thursday, August 29
The Law Offices of Delia Swann.

I am tense. Mom and Dad are being really nice, trying to keep me calm and plying me with interesting snack foods they've gotten from the vending machine down the hall. The miniature chocolate-glazed doughnuts are particularly good, as F.B.s studying the original manuscript of *Lily B.* will note from the smudge of brown icing in the top right corner of this page.

But even chocolate icing cannot change the fact that I am sitting in a law office waiting to give my sworn deposition in the case of White vs. Blennerhassett. Because no matter what happens, whether or not we ever actually go to trial, Delia says I have to tell my story of what happened, which gets written down word for word (verbatim, she calls it), and then I have to sign and swear to the whole story. It occurs to me that it might be simpler if I just handed over my notebook to the lawyers. It's all here, verbatim and everything, with some very nice asides and some perfectly adequate metaphors. But on second thought, I'll just do the deposition and Delia can pay $15.99 for the hardcover edition when it comes out, just like everyone else. And the really pathetic cases like Charlie and Vera, who probably never read books, will just have to wait for the miniseries. (Future Casting

Directors, is it too forward of me to suggest that the role of Lily be played by a young Kirsten Dunst type? And is there any way you could arrange for me to meet Jennifer Aniston?)

I have this strange idea that if I could briefly jump ahead in time and read the next five pages I'm about to write, I'd know exactly what is going to happen. Strange concept. I wonder what would happen if I wrote an entry before an event took place. Would truth subscribe to Lily B.? Would events bend themselves to my creative will?

Well, they're calling my name and I have to go in. I guess that question will have to remain unanswered.

The beanbag chair.

9:48 p.m. Exhausted. But must get it all down. There wasn't time earlier—deposition took two hours; then we went to Italian restaurant. This page will probably still smell like garlic in thirty years.

First I went into Delia's office. My parents had to wait outside. The office was very neat. There was a picture of Ned on the desk and a print on the wall of a man dressed in black in old-time clothes ice-skating. Delia looked very businesslike in her ruthless and yet elegant black suit and power earrings. I felt like I could trust her, and I needed to trust someone, because I was wearing mildly unflattering beige linen pants and a cotton sleeveless top.

Delia told me exactly what would be happening. I would be going with her to a conference room. Vera and her lawyer would be there, too. Charlie would not be there, since he hadn't been injured in the "accident." Delia said there would also be a court stenographer there who would be typing everything we said. Verbatim. I would be questioned by both Delia and Vera's lawyer. I was to tell the truth, simple as that (I've had plenty of practice lately). We got up to go; then Delia put her hand on my shoulder.

"I want to make sure something is clear, Lily," she said. "You are not here to apologize for anything. You are here only to give the facts. Charlie and Vera took advantage of you. They're professionals. But they made a big mistake trying to take advantage of you. You're under eighteen, for starters, so you had no legal right giving them access to that property, and they should have known it. They're not in a great position. It wouldn't surprise me at all to find Vera changing her story. But you let me worry about everything. Just tell your story, and don't let Vera get to you."

I was touched. I had an impulse to hug Delia. But I didn't want to break anything before the deposition, especially my lawyer's bitty bones, so I just smiled and thanked her. And I felt so grateful to her at that moment that I took it upon myself to give Delia a little advice of my own.

"You should open your wedding presents all the way before you send thank-you notes," I said.

"What?" Delia asked, looking blank.

"You thanked my parents for a bird feeder, but there was actually something much better in the box." I told her about the glass pitcher.

Delia slapped her hand to her forehead.

"Oh, how terrible!" she said. "Your mother must have been furious."

"I think she just wants to know you opened the box and got the real present."

Delia leaned forward and squeezed my arm.

"I'll talk to her and apologize. Thank you."

I smiled. "My pleasure."

I took a deep breath, and Delia and I left her office together.

The conference room was ugly. Everything was brown. Vera was already there when I walked in with Delia. She was wearing a black turtleneck and a fancy leather jacket with a wide belt. Her hair was up in a French twist, and she had on big square gold earrings and a matching necklace. It looked like she'd sufficiently conquered her phobia of bathing to clean up for the occasion. She didn't look at me at all. Her lawyer was a tiny guy, an elf in a wide tie, who looked like he might have been out of law school for upward of twenty minutes.

I went first. It was sort of like being on a talk show. Delia asked my full name and address and age. She asked all sorts of questions she knew the answer to, like my parents' names, whether or not they had a second home, where the home was. She asked me to talk about the first time I met Charlie and Vera. I explained how it had happened, how Kay had asked me to sit with them, how her parents had suggested the midnight swim.

Then came some surprises. Delia asked me if I realized that Charlie and Vera had previously known about my parent's lake house and had actually gone to see it on one occasion. I shook my head, and Delia had to tell me to say no out loud, so that the stenographer could record my response. She asked me to recount what Charlie had told me about their house, and I explained about the environmental testing. Then Delia asked if I was aware that there was no house, no testing, that Charlie and Vera rented an apartment (the alleged HTP offices) from which they were, at that time, being evicted for nonpayment of rent. I shook my head again and then remembered to say "no" out loud.

And it went on like this. More stuff they'd lied about coming out. Hug the Planet was nothing more than some stationery and business cards. Charlie and Vera had never done any real nonprofit work at all. I remembered the moldy bologna left at the lake house and began to suspect they weren't even real vegetarians, but that didn't come up. All this time, Vera just sat and stared out the window intently, like she was waiting for a UFO to fly by so she could snap a photograph.

Next, the elf in the wide tie questioned me. He asked a lot of the same things Delia did, but in this dramatic, crafty sort of way like he was expecting to trip me up or something. I guess he'd watched too many episodes of *The Practice* or something, because he always looked like he was about to point a tiny finger at me and shout "AHA!!" But I just told the truth, and the elf had nothing to say about it. When I finished, Delia gave me a smile and a nod, and I knew I'd done okay.

And then, finally, it was Vera's turn. And the elf started asking her questions. And my jaw dropped and my mouth probably stayed wide open for the next hour. Because true to Delia's prediction, Vera lied. Flat-out lied. About everything.

Vera's story:

I had followed her family around at the wedding. They felt sorry for me, and I seemed to be harmless enough, so after repeated badgering, they broke with wedding protocol and allowed me to sit at their table. I had begged their daughter, Kay, to sneak out for a midnight swim, causing them to get into some trouble with hotel management. Against their wishes, Kay had confided to me that they were losing their home. I had informed Kay my family had a perfectly good house standing empty. Kay insisted it would not be proper to discuss it without my parents' approval. I promised to get it.

After the wedding, I made something of a nuisance of myself, showing up frequently at their home and often expecting to be taken out and treated to lunch. They put up with me, again, because they felt sorry for me. And then, to their great surprise, I informed them that my parents had agreed to allow them to stay in the lake house for as long as they needed. And they were so grateful for that. Charlie had specifically requested to meet with my parents in person to work out the details, but I had insisted that was not necessary. So once I handed over the keys, they moved to the lake house and began to settle in.

Then, out of the blue, they received a document from Federal Express requesting them to vacate the premises immediately. They were stunned. They had to pack up and move to a very expensive hotel, because nothing else was available on such short notice. And the timing could not have been worse, because Vera had suffered a very nasty fall in the shower that morning, standing in a tub that could only be described as lethally slick and grabbing for balance at a shelf that had been quite poorly installed.

She had hit her head very hard and was still having double vision when they received the notice requiring them to leave. She still had difficulty turning her head to the right. She was terrified of the shower now, afraid to slip again. They had to take the deluxe penthouse suite at the hotel, though it was far beyond their budget, because it was the only one with a double-size tub and shower with special handgrips. And Vera was simply bewildered with the way the Blennerhassetts had treated them. Why offer their home, only to snatch it away?

The wide-tied elf looked satisfied, and strangely enough so did Delia. I was struck dumb with outrage. I wanted to launch myself over the conference table and grab Vera by the neck, squeezing until her earrings flew off. How could she lie about me so easily, so completely, when I was sitting right there? She obviously felt nothing about me at all. I didn't really exist for her, except as a defendant in a lawsuit.

It was over. Delia took me out to my parents, who were still waiting in the lobby. I hung my head, but Delia told them it had gone very well.

"Vera blew it," Delia said. "I don't think she's used to handling these things without Charlie—he's the brains of the operation. Her story is full of holes, and no judge or jury in their right mind is going to buy it given the Whites' record. Once we've established her testimony as false, the rest will be easy. It's not a sure thing yet. It never is. But I feel very, very good about it. So go home, Blennerhassetts, and try to relax."

Vanessa Lunchmaggot was growing more impressive by the minute. I guess it goes to show you, F.B.s, you really can't judge a book by its cover.

Monday, September 2.
Last two days of summer vacation.

I'm sorry, F.B.s, to have neglected my writing over the weekend. I spent a lot of time with Charlotte, and the rest with my parents. On Saturday they took me to a panel discussion on Chinese porcelain forgeries. It really is a rather fascinating topic. To think a bowl could be worth a half million dollars, then when it turns out that it isn't old at all the very same bowl is only worth a thousand dollars. Imagine paying a half million dollars for something, and then finding out it wasn't what you thought it was. That it was fake. Imagine that.

When I got home from the panel, I found Charlotte had left a photocopied article from the *Harvard Law Review* about the possibility of creating new laws to address the problem of gratuitous lawsuits, with a sidebar essay on the nature of a society that is growing increasingly litigious. (Isn't that just a miraculous word, F.B.s? It means "prone to engage in lawsuits." What a wonderful world that has such words in it.)

There is a lot to be said for an existence that provides nutritious meals, sensible clothes, and periodic exposure to stimulating intellectual subjects, not to mention a best friend who has her finger on the pulse of current American legislation.

I'm not saying I won't ever eat microwave popcorn for breakfast, or leave the dishes on the counter after a meal. I could, one day, go swimming after the pool is closed. I might even, at some point in the future, develop an interest in well-tailored fashion. I just realize, now, that none of this is necessary for me to become a writer. I can be interesting as I am right now. I don't need to stop eating meat, to perform selfless acts just for the sake of "being good." I don't need to write less and do more. I don't need to dress better. (Strike that last one. I DO need to dress better. I just don't need to dress like Karma.) In fact, it's probably better for me to start off simply. That way, there will always be somewhere exciting to go, and there will always be somewhere safe to come home to.

A person just has to do the very best with what she's got. So I will reread that article from the *Harvard Law Review*. I will discuss with my mother how vulnerable we ALL are when it comes to forged Chinese porcelains. And I will listen with my father to the Nitty Gritty Dirt Band, with the volume and the blinds up.

THAT is who I am, Future Biographers. But you probably knew that all along.

Wednesday, September 4
First day of school.

It feels stranger than usual to be back in school, after everything that's happened this summer. It's like the summer in *To Kill a Mockingbird* that brings Dill and Tom Robinson and Boo Radley into Scout's life, and when school finally starts, so much has happened that she will never be the same again. (I would be appalled, F.B.s, to learn a single one of you had not read *To Kill a Mockingbird*. Go, I order you, and pick up that Perfect Novel immediately. After you've finished writing about me.)

It's all history now. The book is closed on Charlie and Vera and Kay White. Except that I still don't have an ending. Nothing to do there but wait.

Friday, September 6
The ending is delivered.

It's all over. I wish I could report firsthand the drama. But sometimes endings are anticlimatic, and I guess this one was. I know only that this morning, while I was at school, Delia stopped by Dad's office with some news.

The Whites have dropped their lawsuit. And now they have dropped out of sight altogether. The wide-tied elf had prepared a document stating that no further claim of any kind would be made by them against my family. Charlie and Vera had both signed it. Dad took his copy and put it away in the file. I would have made copies to include in our Christmas cards, but sometimes the simpler way is the better way.

Delia says we may never know for certain why the Whites dropped their suit. She says she presumes it is because their elf realized that Vera had lied, which is called perjury and not taken at all lightly by the legal system, and that he didn't stand much of a chance of making any money off their case. Or perhaps the insurance company found the case so flimsy they wouldn't offer a settlement. Maybe Charlie had something potentially more lucrative (that means a new scam that would make a lot more money) brewing somewhere else. Whatever the reason, the case has been dropped, and it will never be reopened again.

Is it naïve of me to hope that maybe deep inside Kay feels a little badly about what happened? I mean, obviously Charlie and Vera couldn't care less about me. But does any part of Kay? Did she possibly, ever, at all, enjoy my company? Were there times we had fun that she wasn't faking because Charles had told her to? In spite of her "what-E" act at the mall, is it possible I was her only friend this summer, and she is unhappy about losing me?

Let's not answer the question, F.B.s. Let's just let it sit, in writing, for the world to see. Maybe, if things go my way, Kay herself will read it someday. Maybe.

Sunday, September 8
Szechuan House.

It's my birthday dinner, F.B.s. Although I don't feel I deserve special treatment this year, Mom and Dad said we could go out, along with Charlotte, to any restaurant I wanted. I was kind of leaning toward Pat's Steak Hut, but I know how Dad loves his Szechuan House. Why should he go there only once a year? Why should I not take the tradition on myself? So I made my choice, and everyone seemed delighted.

We're all sitting around the table, eating. Charlotte laughed at the Peking dog joke, and I have to admit it really is very funny when you see those four roasted legs sticking up in the air. When the bill comes, Dad, Mom, and I all say in unison in our best Groucho voices, "This is an outrage! If I were you, I wouldn't pay it!" And Charlotte laughs again, and she looks very pretty in the blue light reflecting off the aquarium. Maybe none of the waiters will drop their trays like they did when Karma walked by, but Charlotte has definitely Got Something.

Even more surprising, as we are having tea and fortune cookies, is that there are presents for me. For a girl who almost bankrupted her family, this is practically unbelievable. I actually feel embarrassed. But Mom and Dad are beaming at each other, and a large present is being produced from under the table, just as the long-suffering Szechuan House waiters emerge from the kitchen with a birthday cake, singing for all they're worth. Everyone in the restaurant is looking at me, and I'm glad. Glad to be there, glad to have my parents and best friend at my table, glad that this is my family. My life.

I blow the candles out and make my wish, and if readers other than my Future Biographers are reading this story in a beautifully bound hardcover or paperback edition published by a major and highly respected New York publishing company, then my wish came true.

Charlotte has a present for me, too, and she asks me to open hers first, because she says it's not as exciting as what my parents got me. It's an envelope, and I open it and pull out a little red-and-white document informing me that Charlotte McGrath has presented Lily Blennerhassett with a twelve-month subscription to *The Economist*. I hug Charlotte and thank her, and tell her that I will try to read every page, especially the ones with pictures. She hugs me back, and everyone is looking, and it is good.

Then Dad gets up and brings the big present around to where I am sitting. He places it carefully in front of me. It looks heavy. Then he retreats to his chair, and the three of them watch me like I'm about to grow a second set of ears.

I rip the paper off all at once, scattering fortune cookies

on the floor in my haste. Then I just sit and stare. I stare, and my eyes blur with tears, and I stare some more, and my mouth moves, but I'm not sure if anything comes out.

Mom and Dad have bought me a laptop computer.

Lily Blennerhasset's Suggested
and Eclectic Reading List
(partial and in no particular order)

The Merlin series by T. A. Barron
Wales, magic, Merlin, Arthur!

The Little House series by Laura Ingalls Wilder
Covered wagons, panthers, pioneer living, adventure!

The Wolves of Willoughby Chase
by Joan Aiken
Mystery, evil governess, runaways, hungry wolves!

Angus, Thongs and Full-frontal Snogging
by Louise Rennison
She's embarrassed! She's in love! She's a diarist! Go, sister!

Interstellar Pig by William Sleator
Games that aren't games, sinister developments,
watch the piggy!

The Dark Is Rising series by Susan Cooper
Age-old prophecies! Deathless evil! Must avoid doom!

A Series of Unfortunate Events series
by Lemony Snicket
Orphans! Endless tragedy! Improve your vocabulary!

Jane's Adventures In and Out of the Book
by Jonathan Gathorne-Hardy
Stare at an illustration and fall in! Try to get out alive!

The Golden Compass by Philip Pullman
England but not England! Daemons! Magic Dust!
A secret journey! Terrifying disturbances!

Joey Pigza Swallowed the Key by Jack Gantos
And I thought I had a lot of energy!

A Wrinkle in Time by Madeleine L'Engle
Space and time travel! Other worlds!
Adventure, sci-fi, fantasy! You will never be the same!

Coraline by Neil Gaiman
Creepy! Sinister! Terrifying!
Grown-ups with buttons for eyes!

The Prydain Chronicles series by Lloyd Alexander
Pig boys, princesses, the Horned King,
and the Cauldron Born! Who will be High King?

Ella Enchanted by Gail Carson Levine
A paradoxical enchantment! A confused conundrum!
How to get out of it?

The Harry Potter series by J. K. Rowling
If you don't already know, I'm not going to tell you.

A Candle in Her Room by Ruth M. Arthur
A doll who enchants and imprisons with malicious intent!
Can anyone break free of her?

A Year Down Yonder by Richard Peck
Grandmother with a rifle! Dungarees! What a life!

Catherine, Called Birdy by Karen Cushman
Medieval diary writer refuses to do what her parents want.
You go, girl!

The View from Saturday by E. L. Konigsburg
Four smart kids and a smart competition.
Who cares if it's a little pretentious? It's a brilliant book!

James and the Giant Peach by Roald Dahl
Cruel aunts, a miserable orphan, an unusual peach,
and some friendly bugs—can they escape?

Harriet the Spy by Louise Fitzhugh
A young writer! Secret diary falls into the wrong hands!
Harriet stands strong!

The Railway Children by E. Nesbit
The country's at war, and Dad is missing!
A new home, exploration, and danger!

Bud, Not Buddy by Christopher Paul Curtis
He's run away! He's written a list!
He's looking for his father! It's jazz, it's travel, it's mystery,
and—while we're on the subject—it's Lily, not Lil.

The Hundred and One Dalmatians (the original novel!)
by Dodie Smith
The real story, so much more amazing than you think!
The drama! The chase!

Holes by Louis Sachar
Scorpions, a missing sneaker, wild onions, and lipstick!
Only a genius could make it work!

The Secret Garden by Frances Hodgson Burnett
Orphaned and angry, but what is the secret
behind the wall? Must find the key!

The Lion, the Witch and the Wardrobe by C. S. Lewis
Truly on of the best books of all time!

A Little Princess by Frances Hodgson Burnett
Those clothes! That doll! An evil headmistress!
And especially that attic!

Charlotte's Web by E. B. White
I knew animals could talk when we're not around!
So good, you'll memorize it.

To Kill a Mockingbird by Harper Lee
The greatest book ever written in the history of the world!
I shall say no more.

The Economist by many smart people
Spinach for the brain (thanks, Charlotte)

Lily B. on the Brink of Cool
Drama! Intrigue! Heartache! Triumph!
Winner of every major literary award in the universe!

ELIZABETH CODY KIMMEL spent her teenage years reading books, watching *Star Trek*, and writing in a purple journal that she fondly named "The Purple Book." Ms. Kimmel is the highly praised author of many books, including *In the Stone Circle*, *Ice Story*, and the Adventures of Young Buffalo Bill series. She lives with her husband and daughter in New York's Hudson Valley and still treasures her multicolored volumes of "The Purple Book."